The Man
Who Would Be
ELVIS

Murdo

*With many thanks
for your sporting cooperation!
See page 23...*

Rick

RICK WILSON

18/11/20

First published in the UK in 2020
by Papingo Publishing
papingopublishing@outlook.com
avenueagency@hotmail.com
Edinburgh EH2 4QW

A CIP catalogue record for this book is available from the
British Library.

This is a work of fiction. Where words have been attributed to
real characters, their permission has been given.

Rick Wilson has been a magazine editor in London,
Amsterdam, Brussels and Edinburgh, where, married to Alison,
he is now a freelance writer, dad of three and grandad of six.
This is his eleventh published book. He has always been an
Elvis fan.

Also by the author:
The Amsterdam Silver
Scotland's Unsolved Mysteries
The Press Gang
Scots Who Made America
The Gemini Enigma
The Man Who Was Robinson Crusoe
The Man Who Was Jekyll and Hyde
The Other Robert
Scotland's Greatest Mysteries
Old Gold

To Freja baby with, as the man would say,
A Big Hunk o' Love

THANKS

For freedom to use their names and professional insights, thanks are due to Scotland's Elvis tribute artists Johnny Lee Memphis (aka John Fleming) and Paul Thorpe; to Johnny's promoter Ken Maybury for his open mind; to Ewan Sinclair for his piping expertise; to those other Sinclairs for their helpful notes; to prison unit manager Steve McCann for showing me around; to Graeme Jessop for his legal advice; to Charlie Berman for our own helpful Boston tea party; and to Go As You Please undertaker Murdo Chambers for thinking out of the box.

Contents

Chapter 1

Real gone daddy

There didn't seem much left of the old man's having-been. Just a dusty Bible and some fairly recent bank statements mixed up with old pension notes, curled-up NHS leaflets on kidney operations, and the occasional faded, black-and-white family photo. All in one tidy pile; by the pillow that still bore the indent of his head.

Once a proud red-haired Scottish warrior, Angus had become boringly grey, genteel and neatly economical towards the end. Too economical to be covered for funeral expenses? It was beginning to look like it, with no insurance documents to be seen. However...

There was one locked wardrobe in the little one-bed unit Roddy Kirkwood's dad had occupied for two years in this rambling Victorian care home on Edinburgh's leafy inner edge. What secrets might that hold?

The son and heir, grieving and aggrieved about his own failing finances, was not expecting much as he began to dig into Angus's non-human remains (the human ones having been already moved). So far, the lad had inherited his dad's befreckled face, ever-puzzled look, ginger hair that reached his chin, and little else. Well, some musical ability. And Shep of course, so called because he was thought to be a German Shepherd before being found to be a high-eared Belgian Malinois.

The bank papers hadn't promised much of a legacy, showing a final credit balance of £74.59 and soon-to-be-stopped state pension payments going out to cover his care as soon as they went in. So surely, thought Roddy, his dad's secret treasures must be hidden away behind this closed door.

Or not...

Elsie McPhee, the home's feisty but sympathetic manager, smiled through her laughter lines as she delved into an apron pocket and handed over the wardrobe key. A smile that said: you'll be lucky, mate. Roddy smiled back with a nod, indicating understanding of the message. Fat chance of any golden goodies here. Always a trim walker but alarmingly skeletal towards the end, Angus had been latterly so frugal he hadn't even claimed his three full meals a day. The pair seemed agreed there would be little to get excited about behind this door.

Now known affectionately as Mama, Elsie hadn't been in charge when the old man joined The Haven's sixty-odd venerables in their comfortable twilight. So she wouldn't know any of his secrets. Nor would Roddy, who in his near-forty years had never had more than superficial thoughts about his dad – admiring his talent and early free spirit which saw him almost emigrating to Canada as a pipe tutor; and his snake-charming of Roddy's fine, now late, English mother Mary. Apart from that inspired acquisition, the old man had never been one for possessions.

And yet...

Roddy turned the sticky key. The wardrobe door was stiff too, so he pushed it inward a little – to hear an agonised squeal from inside. Elsie and he jumped a little, looking at each other in alarm. "What the hell was that?" he said. She just shook a quizzical head.

The door was tentatively pulled back again, allowing some visibility, and there was the scary monster that had made that dreadful noise – a set of bagpipes spreadeagled in all its tentacled glory on the ledge below them. As Roddy blew off some of its dust, it seemed to respond with another blow-back of its own. "Bloody hell," was all he could say as he hugged up its red tartan bag and African Blackwood drones to bundle it, like a groaning baby, into a big black plastic bag.

Further exploration revealed a small – also dusty – record player of Sixties vintage, complete with needled arm, and partly leaning on it a selection of long-play vinyl albums that seemed, on examination, to be caught in a time-warp. The first highly illustrated titles weren't surprising keepsakes for a Scot in his eighties – pipe tunes by the Edinburgh Police Pipe Band; some country dance numbers by long-gone accordion maestro Jimmy Shand, sentimental ballads by the great Caledonian tenor Kenneth McKellar, etc.

But then...

Roddy flicked on further, then... "Eh?" he grunted to no-one in particular as Abba's *Departures* sleeve suddenly appeared. Followed by another couple by the Swedish dancing queens. There were yet more LPs behind these, but, as this archaeological dig was getting challenging, with ranks of hanging clothes inhibiting progress, he decided to remove these before digging further. "I'll take all this to my car," he told Elsie. "Unless there's something another old body could use."

"Doubt it," she said, flatly in her wise no-nonsense way, as she watched Roddy remove well-worn suit after suit, tired shirt after shirt, holed pullover after pullover. "I'd just chuck it all out if I were you," she said, holding up another giant black plastic bag. Just before they both gasped in shock and awe. Suddenly, hoving into full view, came an immaculate full-bodied Highland outfit as worn by the family's grand piper: red tartan kilt and plaid, elaborate doublet, silver-trimmed chain strap and crossbelts, horsehair sporran, spats, feathered bonnet and all.

Roddy carefully lifted out the whole theatrical production, laid it on the floor in all its glory, and stood for a moment in mute wide-eyed admiration, before plunging back into the wardrobe.

The next hanging item, a plain raincoat, covered up something shimmering oddly against the back wall. That looked interesting, but first he should clear the lower shelf to get access. What was behind all those Abba albums? He lifted out all six and went in again to refocus. He couldn't believe his hazel brown eyes as they became accustomed to the dark. The name "Elvis" bounced out at him with the uncovering of every album sleeve, at least a dozen of them, from *Love Songs by Elvis* through *The Essential Presley* to *The Fifty Greatest Hits.*

"My God," he exclaimed.

"What is it?" asked Elsie anxiously, trying not to take full view of his bejeaned behind.

"It's all Elvis stuff. I didn't know... did you?"

"That your dad was an Elvis fanatic? No, I didn't, though he once played us *Love Me Tender* on his pipes on one of our musical evenings. I have to say I found that a bit odd at the time."

"A bit? Pretty damned odd, I'd say." Roddy emerged from the cupboard and started brushing himself down. "The only time he ever mentioned Elvis to me was when he recalled his time in Canada. Said the diner next to his rehearsal studio had nothing but Presley tracks on its jukebox."

Now Elsie had her white-haired head stuck right in the wardrobe. "What on earth?!" she started.

"Tell me," said Roddy, consciously looking away. "Nothing would surprise me now."

Elsie was backing out now, clutching a heavy garment in one hand. It was pure white, matching her hair, heavily sequinned, with a high collar, a big-buckled bejewelled belt, and flared trousers.

"You're going to love this one," said Elsie, adding philosophically: "It's this kind of thing that makes my job here such fun. The old folk's nuthouse." Then she laughed explosively as she saw Roddy remove the hand covering his eyes to take full cognisance of the garment.

"Christ!" he exclaimed. "It's a full-on Elvis outfit. Now I've seen it all."

"Not quite," said Elsie. "There is footwear too." She was raking about the lower drawers, finding a pair of blue slippers, some smart black brogues, a pair of short-legged wellies, and more boots... glamorous cowboy-style ones, designed – she presumed – to go with that white outfit. And now...

"No, you haven't," she said, emerging with something blue in one hand. "You haven't seen it all. At all. How about these..?"

"Suede shoes," said Roddy flatly, as if in a daze. "Blue suede shoes."

"Just don't step on them," said Elsie, dropping them to the floor and chuckling out loud again.

"Fucking amazing," swore the otherwise angelic Roddy; a man of lower middle-class standards who had proudly raised his angelic teenage daughter Lorna with the cleanest tongue in Scotland.

"What did you just say?" Elsie's smiling lips had turned instantly to jaw-dropped shock.

"Er..." Roddy thought quickly. "I said the King was amazing."

"Oh, I thought you said... well, sorry if I misheard and misjudged you."

"That's all right, Mama."

Where had he heard those words before? A mini mono movie of a young Presley singing them flashed across his brain. As if to see it better, he brushed back a handful of slightly greying red hair, then shook his quite-handsome head, while feeling a curl creep into his top lip.

Had the Elvis bug been bequeathed to him?

Little did he suspect it would soon be something to dye for.

Chapter 2

What's it worth?

The family VW Polo seemed to sigh with relief as Roddy and unimpressed help-lad unloaded three huge black bags of bygone just-wearables at Cash4Clothes. Surely there was a handy sum to be got here, whatever they mysteriously did with such stuff? Charity shops wouldn't buy in even while feeling charitable. But this looked like a good place for profitable divestment. To make a start with the funeral fund collection.

Such hopes were soon dashed, however – by the grudging offer of £18; based on sheer recyclable weight rather than the garments' potential for keeping the poor masses warm.

Walking glumly away, Roddy reflected that some of his old man's rejected jackets looked more colourful, if not better, than the grey one he was wearing. Since when had he become so grey? He was once on the edge of long-haired hippiedom, playing in a teenage rock band; now he couldn't even lapse into T-shirt-wearing like his junior store colleagues; he was still a boring white-shirt man, though he'd managed to update his feet in a pair of blue-edged trainers.

He noted a Domino's pizza place next door, and he was hungry. Fiona would be peckish too, soon setting out for work as a night nurse at the Royal. So, before even pocketing it, he handed over the sad yield from Angus's everyday wardrobe in exchange for two £8.99 Sizzlers (sun-dried tomato and garlic sauce, pepperoni, tandoori chicken, onions, jalapeno peppers and herbs). His tears were due to the pungency of the dish, he told himself, as he lustfully munched into one on his disappointed, one-hand-on-the-wheel drive home.

Faithful but faulty, the old automatic jalopy's pale blue hue matched his mood exactly.

Home was superficially brighter: a neat, white-harled Craigentinny bungalow with a little garden and garage in Vandeleur Avenue, less than a mile from the city's reachable beach: Portobello's busy Forth riverside. A modest two-bed-plus-boxroom house to be proud of, though its endless mortgage seemed less modest and more challenging by the month.

On the face of it, he and the handsome, high-cheeked Fiona should never have been utterly hard-up. They were both on a salary, he less regularly than she, admittedly, as he'd never quite found the perfect job for his talents. While managing to keep their love intact, he'd generally failed to live up to her aspirations. One exception being the sending of daughter Lorna to an exclusive – and very expensive – young ladies' school.

Truth be told, that was the killer... or at least the straw that broke the camel's back. Every time something lumpy had to be paid. Poor bloody camel, he would often say to himself.

So far, his requested week off work as a *Morrison's* manager – to sort out his dad's affairs – hadn't gone well. But he still had a few cards up his sleeve. Up the sleeves, indeed, of a couple of more-than-everyday wearables.

And for some unfathomable reason he'd avoid telling Fiona about one of them. As he garaged the car, he heaved the white suit out carefully from the back seat and hoisted it to the back-wall rack, covering it over with his gardening overalls. The piper's outfit was a different proposition. That he left in the car, unpacked and looking like an overdressed invisible passenger, while he went to the house.

Shep barked excitedly on sensing his approach and, despite his eleven years, jumped up like a pup when the door opened. Fiona was sitting at the kitchen table nursing a headache and a decaf coffee. In contrast to the ex-police dog's enthusiasm, she seemed less charmed by Roddy's arrival, even armed with a Sizzler peace offering.

"You know I'm on a gluten-free diet," she said, eyeing the pizza box with disdain. "And I'm late for work, Roderick. Where the hell have you been? You'll have to run us over."

He had often thought of running her over but had never had such a straight invitation. Which was a joke to himself of course; he loved her really...

She was not, however, a bland blonde. Never had been, but was still the sweetest woman in the world beneath a few layers of frustration. These included her endless work on other people's ailing health, giving no time for her own; and her constant feeling that she could have done much better (at least two doctors had been intrigued by her brainy beauty) so why had she fallen victim to the accident and emergency that was Roddy's seed? He never seemed to fulfil his apparent promise; didn't even manage to keep the ambulance driver's job that brought them together. A blue-light crash ended that career. Indeed, although she loved him back in her fashion, she regarded him as a walking, as well as driving, car crash.

If pushed, she might admit to being pleased he was holding down his latest job as a department manager in the local superstore, though he'd never cracked the glass ceiling between him and a comfortable salary. As a couple they were always in financial crisis, always being faced with some unexpected wild card expense blocking the way to a level paying field. And Roddy could tell by her worry lines that one such had turned up today. Asked what it was, she replied...

"The toilet. It's blocked. Not looking at anyone in particular..." her keen blue eyes bored straight into him..."someone has created an incredible nuclear work of nature that won't go away. So stand by for a large plumber's bill."

"What seems to be the trouble?"

"I'm a bit short of clues. Got nothing to go on." A slight smile played across her lips; sometimes she could see the funny side of things.

"But we just got a new cistern along with the revamped system," protested Roddy.

"It's probably not big enough to do the heavy-duty work we, you, require of it. The big one was okay. Why did we change it? You get what you pay for."

"Oh, shit."

"Very aptly put."

He walked into the loo to check it out; tried one failed flush, then found himself half-singing a kind of prayer to the offending unit: "Little cistern won't you do what our big cistern done?"

"Pardon?" said Fiona, hovering behind and referring to the nearby mirror to check her make-up.

"Nothing," said Roddy. "An old song just popped into my head."

"You're nuts. Your brain needs more urgent plumbing than the poo pot."

He took it on the chin, as always. "Anything else troubling you?"

A sigh, hands on hips. "Where should I start? How about the council tax arrears? Or the nagging credit card letters? Or the power company bills? Or your car fuel costs? Or your dog's expensive appetite?" They both glanced over to the kitchen table at the same moment – to see Shep gobbling up the last of the second Sizzler. "Or..."

"Okay, okay," said Roddy, making a calm-down gesture with both hands like an orchestra conductor. "I get the picture. We need some money."

"Doh," she responded while donning her coat and lifting up its frayed hem for inspection. "This is ten years old," she said, "and none of us is getting any younger. Let's go."

Revealing her sweet side for a moment, she hugged the whining old Shep as he was hustled into his crate, then... Roddy was taken aback when his wife headed not for the main door but for Lorna's bedroom, calling: "You ready, honey?"

Why would their daughter be at home? She'd surely be at school. At which point the 17-year-old appeared, not in necktie, school uniform and too-short skirt as expected, but pink of cheek in what looked like climbing gear, overhung by a huge cliff of back-pack.

"Hi Dad," she said cheerily through strands of red hair hiding her bonnie face. "I'm set to go!"

He looked at her with wide eyes. "Where might you be going, young lady?"

"Guatemala," she said flatly.

Roddy coughed with surprise. "Guate-fucking-mala??"

"Please, Dad. Do mind your language." She turned to Fiona. "Didn't you tell him, Mum?"

Fiona directed her answer to him, rather than her. "Have you perhaps forgotten? That your daughter has left school and is now going off on a gap year before studying medicine at university to..." she would make this a real stinging barb..."make up for the failings of her inadequate parents who couldn't manage the full Medical Monty."

"Nobody menioned Guatemala to me," said Roddy defensively, raking his memory. "I believe you said only that she was considering going abroad for a year. Then I heard nothing more ...till now."

"Well, Guatemala is abroad."

Roddy sighed deeply before responding: "Excuse me, ladies, if I acquaint you with some vital facts about that place that I've gleaned over the years. They concern, poverty, local strife, high murder rates..."

"We know all that, Dad," Lorna interjected. "But I'm going to a safe place where an Edinburgh woman has set up a community helping the native people to survive in the mountains."

He knew should have said something like "have a wonderful time", but he heard himself saying only: "You'll miss Grandpa's funeral."

Lorna sighed in the often-exasperated manner of her mother. "I loved my Grandpa but I can't help it if he chose the wrong time to die. My travel has been fixed for ages. He wouldn't mind anyway. He was a great traveller himself, you told me. Once went to Turkey with chicken sandwiches he'd made for lunch there, you said. Or was it to Czechoslovakia with turkey sandwiches?"

"Ha, ha." Roddy tried to laugh but couldn't. Lorna looked

sympathetic and extracted her red-framed iphone from a side-pocket of her backpack.

"Look!" she said, pointing at its screen. "New technology! I can be there on Facetime, or even just make a call to say a few words. Maybe say a prayer for him. Or sing a song."

That thought brought back her dad's smile: "A song would be good."

"OK, which? *Auld Lang Syne* maybe."

"Maybe. Let's decide later."

They all headed silently to the car ...silently until Lorna, having dumped her back-pack in the boot, entered the right-hand rear passenger seat and stood on the plastic bag that still held Angus's squealing bagpipes. She screamed and jumped right back out again. "What the devil was that!"

"Sorry," said Roddy. "I should have warned you about Grandpa's pipes."

As the girl tentatively re-entered, her mum expressed similar shock on taking the front passenger seat with a backward glance. "And what the hell's *that*?" she asked, registering the piper suit spread all over Polo's back seat.

"It's a piper suit," said Roddy. "Once worn by Dad. In his glory days."

"Thank God for that," she said. "I thought it was a real Highlander about to cut my throat with his sgian dubh."

Three minutes later, having thought about it, she asked: "Why have we got it here?" She had forgotten momentarily that Roddy had been earlier at the care home.

"It's to pay the old man's funeral expenses," he offered.

"What? Why? Didn't the miserable old bugger have that covered? No insurance? No money in the bank? No other willing relatives? Is that what you're telling me?"

"I reckon so," said Roddy sheepishly. "There was nothing

else to be found in his room, except a bank statement for £74.59."

"Oh, bloody hell...You mean seeing him off is all down to us?"

"Seems like it."

She sighed all of her breath out, realising that a dead man's bank balance was still healthier than theirs. "And pensions? How about his pensions? He must have been saving these up."

"I fear not, dear." Roddy's nervous right foot plunged too heavily on the accelerator and the car lept forward. A sharp reminder of his career-changing ambulance crash; just to add to the drama. Fiona gasped, as he went on...

"As an only-occasionally-employed pipe tutor, he was clearly one of the original victims of the gig economy. With nothing permanent to show for it."

"But the state pension... he must have been getting that?"

"Talking about new technology..." Roddy pulled up behind a maroon Lothian Region bus at a traffic light, winked at Lorna, took his own newish Smartphone from a top pocket, clicked to a site he'd checked earlier, and passed it to Fiona. Who read...

You still get Basic State Pension if you move to live in a care home. However, if your care home fees are paid in full or part by a local authority, NHS or out of any other public funds, you may have to use your State Retirement Pension to pay a contribution to the cost of care.

She sighed again. "So that's that. Whatever money he got went straight into his care bill. And as his death will now have been intimated to the Pension Department, there won't be any more in the pipeline."

"Or even the bagpipe line," Roddy tried to joke. It was ignored.

"Leaving the big question: Where are we supposed to get the money? If we don't intend to dump him in a ditch."

"Well, as I say, there's always his old Highland kilt outfit..." Roddy pointed a raised thumb at the back seat. "Must be worth something. I checked out the value of the full shebang new... it's about £2,500."

"New maybe. Preloved maybe not," said Fiona. "Even trying to sell online, which there's no time for anyway."

"It's still in good nick. The old man treasured it, I'm sure. We can try selling it in town."

They were passing Holyrood High School on the left and skirting the dramatic volcanic hills of the Royal Park on their right, heading up towards Craigmillar Castle and beyond. "It's a pretty sellable Scottish image for visitors," said Roddy. "People all over the world go for it."

"Aye, maybe," said Fiona in an exaggerated Scottish accent as the car descended through a strip of woods behind which the modern all-white hospital complex nestled. "What's the current cost of arranging a funeral? Five thousand maybe. Even if you sell the stuff for a good figure, the sums will never add up."

"Don't worry," said Roddy. "I have an idea to pull it off."

"In a few days? I'll believe that when I see it," she added, sweeping open the car door on arrival. "We're going to have to sell this old rust bucket or take in a lodger to fill this lass's empty room."

Tears suddenly sprung freely from her eyes as she leaned into the back and grasped her daughter tightly. "Have a wonderful time, darling," she said, "and make sure you come back to us."

"Bye, Mum," was the simple reply. But the young voice was shaking... with trepidation, love and excitement.

* * *

In the unmoving car, a pregnant silence followed Fiona's disappearance through the hospital's staff entrance. Until Lorna finally addressed her thoughtful father: "You can take me to the station now, Dad."

He woke with the realisation of another looming goodbye: "You flying from London?"

"Yup."

"Where to again?"

"Guate-fucking-mala," said the angelic one, who seemed suddenly to have lost her wings.

They laughed all the way to Waverley Station.

Chapter 3

A fit of coffin

"No problem," said the youthful funeral director, scanning the mono photo of a boyish Angus at full kilt – with pipes you could almost hear skirling across the years. A magnificent image, evoking his enemy-scaring marches on the killing fields of Korea. Just perfect to illustrate his coffin through the good offices of Go As You Please. "We can certainly have that blown up and attached."

Go As You Please was all for new and exciting ways to meet one's maker. With six centres down south, it had just branched out to Scotland with novel window displays – coffins festooned with illustrated evidence of the occupant's enthusiasms, be it wine, women or song – that had lately caught Roddy's passing eye.

All in all, a cheaper, cheerier style. And cheaper was the preferred word for Roddy, in view of family funds being seriously limited even before the absence of any contribution from the star of the show. He had already won a money-raising delay by phone, being assured a cheque was acceptable.

Now at the shop in person, however, he had another little request...

The basic biodegradable coffin's price was £300. Adding a picture, in a digitally applied vinyl wrap, brought the tag up to £500. A bit of a luxury! So would a second photo add more to the coffin cost? Murdo Chambers looked sympathetic. "Don't worry about that," he said solemnly. "We'll just add it as a goodwill gesture. We are people of genuine empathy; we're not just about the money.

"A close relative, is it? His wife? Yourself maybe?"

Roddy handed over the second picture with a pink flush of embarassment. "Actually it's..."

"Elvis!" said a wide-eyed Chambers, accepting what a moody cut-out image from a magazine. He spluttered into his tea and, after a fit of coughing, slapped a hand over his mouth to hide its wetness and restrained laughter. "I take it *he* wasn't a friend of the family?"

"Not exactly," said Roddy, "but Dad was a big fan."

"A Scottish bagpiper who was also a big Elvis follower? That's a pretty unusual combination, I'd venture to say, sir."

"I know. It surprised me too. So you won't do it?"

Despite riding this new goodbye wave, the young man regarded Roddy with an old undertaker's studied sympathy. "We pledge to let the client do whatever he or she wants. So long as their requests aren't too far beyond bizarre and don't affect the quality of service. So of course... I don't know about your dad, but I reckon Elvis was – is – real quality. I confess! I'm a fan too. He'll be up there in lights on the front of the coffin, just where he belongs, at no extra charge. Looking upwards to Heaven but also up to your dad. However..."

"However?"

"What about words? Was your dad religious at all? I know Mr Presley was a believer."

"Yes, I believe Mr Kirkwood was too. In his way..."

Chambers tapped a pencil on his tea cup. "Something simple but meaningful, a short headline suggesting respect and hope on the other side. But maybe also suggesting mutual admiration."

"But Elvis couldn't possibly have known Angus or his work."

"A mere detail," said Chambers, a smile breaking on to his face. "Both were fine musicians in the same era." He winked under his Lennonesque glasses, pushed the pencil into his desk and grimaced as it broke in half. "I think I've got it."

"Yes? Pray tell."

"One of the King's greatest tracks. *How Great Thou Art.* Just these four words spread across both pictures. No more words, only these. Class, eh? What d'you think?"

"Can't say I know the song."

"No? Hang on a minute..." The casually dressed, open-necked undertaker coughed a little, before vanishing into the darkness of his back shop to emerge with a battered old Spanish guitar. He handed it to Roddy in the full expectation that musical ability ran in the family blood – before dialling the song up on his phone and singing along with the King, in a surprisingly deep, not-unpleasant voice...

And then proclaim, my God, how great Thou art
Then sings my soul, my saviour God to Thee
How great Thou art, how great Thou art...

"Brilliant," said Roddy, who had quickly corrected the instrument's tuning, found a couple of chords from the memory of his teenage band days, and sung along a little. "That's class indeed. The old man would have approved."

"Keep the guitar," said Chambers as he rose with a toothy smile, bowed a little and held out a written cost estimate. "You can obviously use it. I can't. A client's long-forgotten prop. His folks reckoned it wouldn't be needed on his journey but didn't bother to collect it."

"You're too kind," said Roddy, glancing at the proffered sheet. It included all the details, such as a rural wooded venue, a minister to give the eulogy, flowers, a piper tribute act, solemn diggers, and portable speakers for any songs to be sung. The bottom line said £3000 and he sighed with relative relief as he pulled out a tattered cheque book. Not an unreasonable price, he thought, for such a nice, if sad, moment.

He signed with a little flourish. But as he left the shop with the old guitar still slung across his chest, his satisfaction was muted by the urgent challenge of finding the cash to cover the cheque before it hit the bank.

And by the sight of two men carrying a wrapped-up human body from a Ford Galaxy (dead) people-carrier into the back entrance.

Chapter 4

Tartan of a Titan

This wasn't the Morrison's he was familiar with. Nestled near the John Knox House on the Royal Mile, John Morrison's window display was festooned with tartans arranged around the bold focal point of a headless, kilted military figure in a bright red tunic. The shop proudly proclaimed itself a kiltmaker and weaver ...and who could be more interested in buying the old man's full-scale piper suit?

"Well, sorry, not us," said the tweed-jacketed kilted manager Iain Mackie, framed between ranks of more tartan creations. "It's just not the sort of package that gets bought in second-hand – by any high street specialists. Your best bet is to go online with it."

"No time," said an agitated Roddy, who kept glancing behind himself. "In more ways than one. My car is on a fast-expiring parking ticket."

"So sorry, sir..."

"Can you at least take a look at it and tell me what prices I might ask for the various bits online?"

To his credit, the ruddy-faced manager didn't sigh, though he looked ready to. "Okay, just bring it in so I can take a look," he said. He was accustomed to foreign heritage nutters with odd requests, but this – being a native – was particularly odd.

While Roddy got his mobile calculator ready, the whole outfit was laid across his counter and, one by one, the expert went over the possible prices he felt could be achieved online.

"It's fine quality, no doubt, but used is used," he said. "Nevertheless, the doublet could fetch maybe £300, the sporran £200. I'd put £100 on the plaid, £50 on the crossbelts, £200 on the sgian dubh and maybe £150 for the feathered hat. But the kilt is the most interesting item of course, which would probably fetch about £350. What's the family tartan?"

"I suppose it's Kirkwood," said Roddy, who now had a sum of £1350, "though I'm ashamed to say I've never checked to see if I'd like to wear the design myself."

"Let's see then," said Mr Mackie, producing a cloth book-like guide to tartans...and failing to find a Kirkwood matching the kilt's checks. Though both were assertively red, the squares of the chosen page were much the tighter of the two. "Might there be another family name of relevance?"

The idea just popped into Roddy's head. "I know it sounds daft but... Presley perhaps."

"As in Elvis?"

"Uh-huh," he found himself grunting in a distinctly Elvis fashion. "But maybe with a slightly different spelling."

"Yes, I've heard his ancestors may have come from Scotland. Let's try it..."

"Just a sec," said Roddy. "Let me confirm that." He regeared his mobile phone, called up Google and typed into it "Elvis Presley's Scottish background". And...what a coincidence! An old BBC News release popped up, featuring the words and experience of yet another Morrison...

Elvis roots lead to Scotland

Elvis Presley's roots can be traced back to a village in Aberdeenshire, according to a Scottish author.

Allan Morrison, from Greenock, has discovered that the musical icon's ancestors lived in Lonmay in the 1700s.

"I am an Elvis fan myself so it has been a joy to trace back their past and establish that the Presleys were of Scottish origin," he said. "When I got the family tree back to Lonmay it was like striking gold."

The Presley roots in America could be traced right up to 1933, when Elvis's parents married. The singer was born two years later.

Scotland was also the location for The King's only visit to the UK, a brief landing at Prestwick Airport in 1960.

Scrolling on, Roddy noted another more recent entry, based on a feature by Gayle Ritchie for the Aberdeen *Press & Journal*, which was even more illuminating:

Andrew Presley, who was Elvis's great-great-great-great-great-great-grandfather, emigrated to North Carolina in 1745 and started the American branch of the family.

According to the parish register, records showed that Andrew Presley's father, also Andrew, married Elspeth Leg in Lonmay on August 27, 1713.

The Presleys would have been married at the village's old parish church, built in 1607 but now a ruin. It lies just outside the estate of Cairness, a former seat of the Gordons with a fine mansion house.

Nine of their children were recorded in the register, but there was a tenth son, Andrew, born about 1720, who made his living as a blacksmith and left Lonmay for Anson County, North Carolina, in 1745.

The Presleys' story is a classic tale of emigration – from rags to riches within six generations.

The two men looked at each other, both mouthing a silent "wow" before returning to the tartan trail. A few more flicks of the guide's cloth pages produced the goods. Under various spellings of the surname – Pressly, Preslie and Presley – there appeared a broad-checked, red-accented tartan emanating from Aberdeenshire and looking like a match with that lay across the shop counter.

The guide page and the kilt were brought together and both men stared at both things in amused disbelief. Then the shop man said: "So the old piper wore a tartan in honour of the Presley family's original home, if not to honour the great man himself? I assume he was something of a fan."

Roddy nodded. "You could say that. In fact, it's beginning to look like he was kind of obsessed. But would the Presley connection maybe tempt you to buy?"

"Doubt it," said the manager. "But I'll check with the boss. Might propose paying you half those suggested online values. But it's up to him. Let me make a call."

Respecting the call's privacy, Roddy stepped back and looked out into the rainswept street. There, with his back on view as he leant over the Polo's windscreen to attach a parking fine, was a Yellow Meanie, as he knew parking attendants. Blood surged to his head, he whirled back, grabbed the sgian dubh from the piper outfit and charged into the street. Was he going to kill this man with the silver dagger? He asked himself. Surely not, he told himself. He saw himself appearing in court already, saying: "I only meant to frighten him, your honour." He let out a roar that didn't sound like a word, and the attendant turned to face him.

With a big smile.

She was the prettiest thing he had seen all day. So pretty he dropped the knife and smiled back. "Sorry," he said, as – again – a song surged through his head. It wasn't an Elvis one this time. It was a Beatles one well remembered as his own rock group, of wild teenage drinkers, had been cleverly dubbed The Bottles. "Lovely Rita, meter maid..." Another big smile came as she said "Sorry, sir" and he picked up the offensive weapon, pretended it was a pen going into his pocket, and retired again with mixed feelings to the shop.

What was the verdict?

"No sale, I'm afraid," said Mr Mackie. "But the boss says we can perhaps hold it for you and try to find a buyer if you like. In which case we would charge twenty per cent."

Roddy retrieved the dagger and resisted the urge to scare him with it, as he handed it over and said without enthusiasm: "Ok. You'll need this bit too."

Now everything depended on the bagpipes.

Chapter 5

Pipes to the tune of...

Scrunch upon squeaking scrunch. Rolling down the Royal Mile with wipers rhythmically shredding the unremoved parking fine, he slowed down by a statue of the poet Robert Fergusson. A life-size selfie target for amused Japanese visitors who probably didn't know he died at 24... but not before inspiring the other great Robert...Burns. Who had expressed his thanks by digging the boy up from a pauper's grave and buying him a headstone with dedicated poem.

But who could rescue Angus from such a fate? Did they even do paupers' communal graves these days? Who? Well, it had to be Roddy. There was no-one else. He pulled the Polo's fading handbrake, slid down the front passenger window, and addressed the oddly animated figure: "Gonna inspire me too, pal?" Holding a book in his right hand, his thumb was raised in a gesture that seemed to say: "You can do it, my friend!"

Thus encouraged, Roddy drove on with a new breeze behind him, as well as a honking, impatient traffic queue.

* * *

Next stop: the famous bagpipe-maker William Sinclair, established in 1906 and occupying an elegant, old-fashioned corner of Madeira Street in Leith. The original William was no more, and the third had just gone; but Ewan was now holding the fort. With such a lineage, he was bound to have a good idea of bagpipe values, just so long as it wasn't the tatty £20 pieces of nonsense sold to tourists. And if Angus's was a good set – which was likely – there would surely be some money in it. Maybe even enough to augment a £2000 yield from the car; to reach the £3000 funeral fee.

"We don't usually buy in from individuals," said the bearded Ewan, fronted by his counter and backed by photos of his venerated forebears. "But maybe I can help put a value on it. The best examples from the olden days can fetch a fair bit of money. Especially from the days before the 1990 ivory ban when..."

"How much are we talking about?" asked Roddy, his eyes widening with anticipation, his sweat-wet fingers slipping off the pipes' black-bag packaging held tightly to his body to stop it falling.

"Well, obviously it depends on age, the maker's name, quality, condition, all that sort of obvious stuff. But the value can go impressively high."

"How impressively?"

Ewan chuckled a little at Roddy's agitation and couldn't resist the KO punch. "Well, I have a set in the back shop – bequeathed to me by my grandad as life insurance, he said – that was made by the legendary MacDougal of Breadalbane in the mid-1800s and is now worth at least..."

He paused for the fun of it, while Roddy urged him on.

"At least..?"

"At least £10,000."

The plastic bag fell to the ground with a clatter, just as Roddy's bottom lip fell with an odd squeak.

"Have a care," said Ewan, holding a muscular hand out. "Better pass it over and let me have a look before you do any more damage."

Tenderly, as if picking up a newborn baby, the expert gathered the whole concoction of maroon woollen bag, silver mouthpiece, bass and two tenor drones, ivory mounts and ferrules, and held them out before himself for keen-eyed examination. "Quality," he said after perhaps half a minute. "There is a wonderful finesse to the turning of the drones' wood. It could be made by..."

"Someone special?"

"I suspect it's a Peter Henderson job and you don't get more special than that. Especially if it can be dated to the peak time of the man himself working in Glasgow between 1888 and 1875." Ewan up-ended the set and drew Roddy's attention to its silver mountings. "Indeed, there's no doubt about it. Look here."

There was the distinctive Glasgow hallmark, lion rampant, thistle and date – 1870 – along with the initials PH.

"That's good then?" asked Roddy tentatively, not daring to believe that it was.

"Good? I think you've struck gold."

"Gold?" He was wiping the excitement from his brow. "How much gold would you say?"

"Ballpark maybe £5,500."

Roddy, gasping, had to grip the edge of the counter to stop himself slipping to the floor, as Ewan added...

"For which I might break our no-buy rule. If you want a

quick deal, I'd offer you £5,000 today, leaving myself some leeway for profit. I might have a customer in mind."

This was a no-brainer. Roddy extended a hand for shaking, but Ewan held back. "Of course, it all depends how it sounds. It ought to be extremely sweet, but you never know. Let me just test it."

He rubbed a wipe over the mouthpiece and went into the back shop to find favourable accoustics. Roddy, uninvited, listened intently from the front shop, finding it too close to tolerate the usual preparatory squealing. But to his surprise, the subsequent rendering of *Flower of Scotland* didn't sound much better.

A disappointed-looking Ewan re-emerged saying, "Not good. There's something far wrong. It could be a blockage."

He laid the set on the counter again and started examining the drones. The bass one didn't look right. Where there should have been darkness there was white. Was that a piece of paper? He found a safety pin and started poking delicately into the pipe. Yes, it was paper, coming out gradually in a tight roll. He unrolled it a little, noting it was lined, as if from a school exercise book, and that there was hand-writing on it. Also the name of an addressee. "I think it's for you," he said, handing it over to an astonished Roddy, who unrolled it some more before reading with wide eyes...

Hello Roderick

I knew you would get here eventually. You were always a clever lad. These pipes are my pride and joy, worth a lot, so they should pay for my fond farewell. If there's any left, please keep half as a goodbye kiss from me to you, Fiona and your lovely Lorna, and be kind enough to send the other half to the bank number on the back of this paper (an old debt). Thank-you for being a great son. In the words of the song,

Maybe I didn't love you quite as often as I could have. But you were always on my mind. Proud of you to the end.

Your Loving Daddy

Angus

PS: Please have Amazing Grace played for me, just to recall my wretched life and my amazing visit to Memphis. Did I ever tell you I'd been to Graceland? Silly old bugger that I was...

Graceland?! Thinking that would have once surprised him, Roddy flipped over the paper and noted the easy-to-remember sort code...60 80 09... but not the long account number. Who on earth could this be, and where? He'd check it out of course, but there wouldn't be much point bothering if the pipes refused to deliver the goods.

"Is the blockage cleared now?" he asked the pipe expert.

"Reckon so," said Ewan. He didn't bother to re-enter the back shop for testing; just had another good blow that delivered the required melody with the expected sweetness. His big smile said it all.

"Deal on?" queried Roddy, still a touch insecure.

"Deal on," said Ewan. "I'll see the money is transferred today."

Roddy hadn't done that back-heel kicking thing for a couple of decades. But now he did it again, better than he'd ever done it in boyhood, as he returned to the car he wouldn't have to sell after all.

Chapter 6

Back to nature

Why does it always rain on me? Roddy wondered glumly as ice-cold raindrops merged with the emptying of leaves above him …on to his hatless head, over his already-tearful eyes, down behind the black tie into his freezing back. Everyone else seemed better prepared with brollies at full stretch. Not that "everyone" added up to much of a gathering for Angus's final farewell in the little copse above an isolated rural hill in the Borders.

Still shivering, though, were an elegantly black-costumed Fiona on a rare day off, the kilted piper set to play Angus out, the grave digger, a small busload of five pensioner-friends from the care home, their "Mamma" Elsie, the funeral director, the minister briefed by the son to talk about the father; and a silent, silhouetted woman who had arrived in a black cab.

The cardboard coffin was lying beside its hole as the first group drew nearer to it. Shep, also an honoured guest, ran forward to start circling it and whining in apparent distress: was he recognising the scent of his last-but-one master (Angus had rescued him from a predeceased police dog-handler friend) or was he reacting to the image on the box?

Fiona was certainly reacting to it. Closing in to calm and gather the dog, she looked down at the coffin with astonishment. Given that she hated the undignified idea of illustrated coffin lids, she could almost accept the fine study of her father-in-law in full tartan pipery; what put her into full shock was the accompanying portrait of Elvis Presley. A golden belt sliced across both pictures at 45 degrees, bearing in bright red the words *How Great Thou Art*.

She grabbed Roddy by the elbow. "Have you seen this?" she demanded in a stage whisper, adding before he could even nod: "Was this your doing?"

"I got two pictures there for the price of one," said Roddy wiping rain and tears from his face. "I thought he'd like it."

"Why in God's name would he have liked it?" The tone of Fiona's face was turning from pale to a purple hue. "It's pure kitsch. What on earth has Elvis Presley got to do with it?"

"Because, believe it or not, Dad was an Elvis fan." Roddy couldn't resist a slight smile as he broke the news to the old man's buttoned-up daughter-in-law.

"Don't talk rubbish," she protested. "Angus was a traditional, old-school Scottish musician, and a very fine one at that. I don't know how you can dishonour your own father like this."

Just then, the piper, who had claimed a brief friendship with Angus, began playing one of the old man's most beautiful self-composed pipe tunes, *Lord McPherson of Drumochter*.

"There's the evidence of it," she said. "Fine music of great cultural dignity. Evocative of our hills, heather and heritage. What evidence have you found to support the idea that your father was some kind of old gum-chewing rocker?"

"Shhh, my dear," said Roddy, putting a finger to his mouth and urging silence. They listened respectfully, proudly aware of the music's cultural significance. Until...

Suddenly and cleverly, the piper changed his tune, and in so doing caused Fiona to almost change hers. The melody slipped seamlessly from *Lord McPherson* to the King's classic *Are You Lonesome Tonight?*, a move greeted with a smattering of applause from the older guests.

"There it is," whispered Roddy. "His piper friend obviously knew his secret too."

Fiona turned away, shaking her head silently, as the tributes began. She jerked the agitated dog to heel when the minister began speaking – warm but well-practised words that did not really reflect Angus's complex character. More sincerely, Roddy then spoke of his love and admiration for his well-travelled, music-loving father, who – he revealed to the audible surprise of all – had been a devoted fan of the man from Graceland. Which prompted the piper to launch into *Amazing Grace*.

Then praises were literally sung. For which Roddy had brought along his newly acquired guitar. Right on cue, the lovely Lorna rang in, all the way from sun-kissed Guatemala City. She smiled into her dad's phone screen, which he circled around the gathering as her sweet voice sang Robert Burns's *Ae Fond Kiss*, and the gathering gradually joined in. She concluded with the spoken words "Goodbye, my dear Grandpa. I will always love you", then signed off with a thrown kiss.

Roddy decided to close it all with an equally meaningful song. One that had meant a lot to Elvis, and presumably also to his here-present admirer. With the help of YouTube, *Take My Hand Precious Lord* had been well practised – in the garage – for the last couple of days, and he projected it out with all the depth and tonal qualities of the man himself.

Precious Lord, take my hand
Lead me on, let me stand
I'm tired, I'm weak, I'm lone
Through the storm, through the night
Lead me on to the light
Take my hand, precious Lord,
Lead me home

As he sang, the minister, grave-digger, funeral director and piper stepped forward to lower the coffin into the ground. A typical order of service would have required more philosophical expressions of life, death and mourning, but when he finished, there was a tearful-but-cheerful "That's all, folks" from Roddy before the mourners began to break up, shake his hand, and wander thoughtfully back to their cars. One of which was a black cab with a bored-looking driver reading a newspaper.

Roddy saw the mysterious woman walking towards it. Dressed in an elegant grey coat and black wide-rimmed hat above a dark veil, she had held discreetly back during the tributes, almost hiding behind one of the trees. He glimpsed the newspaper her driver had been reading above the dashboard. *The Nottingham Post.* Who did he know in that city? And why would they come all the way here by taxi?

It was probably an English someone who must have read *The Scotsman* death notice; so an English someone who cared a fair deal about Scotland, and clearly about Angus in particular.

She looked a touch over forty. Who on earth was she? Why had she appeared here? He had to know. He decided to step forward, catch her up and get some answers before the cab left...

But just as he set off, Mama Elsie grabbed him from behind. "I didn't know you could sing like that," she told him. "Like

Elvis indeed. Incredibly so, if I may say."

"Hey, that's nice of you to say so, but..." he laughed.

"I couldn't tell the difference! How d'you like to come and entertain us at The Haven? As Elvis. A tribute to him and your dad. Maybe once a week. Just for fun. Well, maybe for more than fun. How about £60...?"

"Oh, I don't know about that," he repeated; but he did know. It wasn't the thought of limited stardom that excited and delighted him. It was the thought of the money.

"I'll think about it," he said, "and I'll call you. But excuse me for a minute."

He resumed his pursuit of the grey-coated, middle-aged woman. But she was now in the back of the cab, setting off down the hill. She had removed her veil and he caught a glimpse of her face as she swept past and glanced back. There was something familar about it.

Another Angus secret, he wondered, as he walked back through the trees to his own car. Where Fiona and dog were awaiting him and his key. "What did the care home lady want to talk to you about?" she asked.

"Oh, nothing," he said and didn't know why he said it. "She was just saying how much she'd miss Dad."

"We all will," she said as she bundled a rain-soaked Shep into the back seat. "But did we really know him?"

"I'm not sure about that, honey," he said thoughtfully. "Not sure at all."

Chapter 7

Rock of Ages

Phew. After all the sadness, he felt uplifted here. Was he in his true element? With its low ceilings and subdued drum-cymbal lights, the Hard Rock Cafe on George Street was an oddly contradictory harbour of peace and rocking ravery. It wasn't too busy, pop videos were pumping away from all corners, Joe Cocker was singing for help from his friends, and there were scores of wall-mounted reminders of, well, not the Rock of Ages (which he should have been thinking about now) but the Ages of Rock.

Roddy ordered a flat white, but rather than sit quietly awaiting it, wandered around the tables and walls well-hung with rock 'n' roll memorabilia, much of in elaborate frames – a chainmail jacket worn by Ringo Starr for a photo shoot; Pete Townsend of The Who's angular Gibson Flying V guitar; a 1969 Woodstock poster; Jimi Hendrix's airline ticket for a 1970 London-New York flight; a waistcoat worn by Monkee Davy Jones; portraits of The Beatles, Blondie, and – of course – The

King. There was not only an autographed portrait of Elvis but an actual sombrero worn by him in the 1963 movie *Fun in Acapolco*.

Of course, the not-so-great pretender shouldn't have been here at all. The post-burial plan, suggested by Elsie of the care home, had been for mourners to retire to her establishment's dining room for tea and cakes. But it was Elsie herself who had called it off, saying: "I'm sorry, love, but my people are very tired after the trip and all; so if you don't mind, we'll just call it a day." Roddy returned an apparent smile of thanks and sympathy which was really one of relief, then of mild excitement, as she added: "Don't forget my offer. We'd love to have you for a musical evening."

He nodded, trying not to look as interested as he felt.

When he told Fiona of the call-off, she too was relieved, happy to have a quiet Friday evening at home for a change. So Roddy felt free to follow his own star... find somewhere for a final, non-alcoholic toast to Angus, now off to join his heavenly hero. So it had to be at the Hard Rock Cafe, he reckoned, as he was about to don the persona of that hero, the world's greatest-ever rock icon, no less. If only for one night maybe next week for a few decrepit old ravers. If only for £60.

He'd decided to be bold; forget his natural shyness and accept Elsie's offer. Because in the end it wouldn't be him anyway; he'd be protected by being someone else. He could always blame Elvis for any screw-up in his performance. What did it matter anyway? It was hardly the Carnegie Hall.

Rocking with the oldies would be at least a refreshing change from the mundane regularity of his daily work. Daily work! The thought of it had already given him the Monday morning blues. Even before the weekend. He knew he wasn't too bad as the superstore's fruit-and-veg manager – one of seventeen department managers, no less – and believed the company thought that too. But he had to admit to himself (if not to them) that retail work was really not his forte at almost forty. He missed the excitement that had so coloured his youth with The Bottles, and his later young life with the siren-screaming ambulance service.

The flat white arrived. He took a long sip of it, surveying again all the fun of the cafe's walls as he did so; the guitars and posters and oddly meaningful trivia of the business he was about to rejoin in a very minimal fashion. One displayed item, a roughly printed magazine page from the early 1960s – headed *"The complete lowdown on America's No 1 singing star"* – offered all that he, or anybody, needed to know about the genesis of the man he would now (pretend to) be. It read...

Real name: Elvis Aaron Presley
Date of birth: January 8, 1935
Birthplace: East Tupelo, Mississippi
Mother's name: Gladys Smith
Father's name: Vernon Elvis Presley
Brother: Twin Jesse Garon Presley (died at birth)
Height and weight: 6 feet, 185 pounds
Color of eyes: Hazel
Marriage status: Single
Religion: Protestant
Schools: L. C. Hume High School, Memphis, Tennessee
Closest friends: Red West, Gene Smith (cousin), Charles Neal
Favorite clothes: Sharp sport clothes, draped jackets, bright colors, hand-made lace shirts
Favorite colors: Pink and black
Favorite foods: Pork chops with gravy and mashed potatoes; hamburgers
Nickname: "The Cat"

Favorite type of car: Cadillac

Favorite drink: Plain ice water

Brand of cigarettes: Doesn't smoke

Hobbies: Dating, motocycling, waterskiing, movies, billiards, collecting records

Favorite sports: Football, boxing

Favorite actors: Marlon Brando, Rod Steiger, James Dean, Glenn Ford, John Wayne

Favorite actresses: Natalie Wood, Doris Day, Kathryn Grayson

Favorite singers: Bing Crosby, Perry Como, Frank Sinatra, Dean Martin, The Four Lads

Favorite comedians: Steve Allen, Milton Berle

Reading matter: Motion picture magazines

Former occupations: Theater usher, truck driver, factory worker

Present home town: Memphis, Tennessee

People who've helped him: Sam Phillips, Bob Neil, Tom Parker, Bill Black, Scotty Moore

Favorite music: All kinds – country, pop, jazz, blues, gospel, rock and roll

Instruments played: Guitar

Recording companies: Sun, now RCA Victor

Best-selling record: Heartbreak Hotel

Other records: That's All Right, I Forgot to Remember, Blue Suede Shoes, Baby Let's Play House, Good Rockin' Tonight, Milkcow Blues Boogie, Tutti Frutti, I Got A Woman, Blue Moon, Just Because, I Was The One, I Want You, Hound Dog.

Quite a take-off, thought Roddy. Not bad for a one-time truck driver. Talent just had to float up from the depths of simple beginnings to the Fame Sea's sun-kissed surface. Getting into the spirit of it, he unbuttoned his white collar, loosened both black tie and tongue, and grunted "Uh huh," in true deep Elvis fashion.

"Pardon?" said an equally deep nearby voice.

"Oh, sorry," said Roddy as his eyes wandered to a more close-at-hand scene...in which the male half of the trendy-looking couple at the next table was reading the *Daily Express:* surprisingly uncool in such a place, he thought. "I didn't say anything."

But his eyes widened in shock as they took in a headline on the main City & Business page. He stretched over to get a better view of the fateful words *Morrisons axes 3,000 managers,* while annoying the estate agent type and his hot property by his very proximity.

"Here, you can have it," said the irritated uncool dude, surrendering his paper. "We were just leaving anyway."

"Thanks," said Roddy, accepting the offer. "Looks like I will be too."

"Pardon?"

"Oh, nothing." He focused in on the news piece and further loosened his black tie as he read:

Morrisons plans to axe 3,000 management jobs in a major overhaul of its store operations that will see thousands of staff recruited for shopfloor roles.

The UK's fourth biggest supermarket is creating 7,000 new hourly paid roles for its 492 stores.

This will mean a net 4,000 extra staff taken mainly to fill positions across the Market Street counters where skilled butchers, bakers, fishmongers and other fresh food specialists serve customers.

All stores will retain an overall manager but departmental roles in areas such as beers, wines, and spirits will be cut. Affected managers will be able to move to the new jobs, but there will be "a short period of uncertainty for some", according to the group retail director.

* * *

He gulped down his coffee then stood up with new energy. Or was it panic? Before leaving the cafe, he felt guided by an odd impulse into a big display of Hard Rock Cafe T-shirts near the door. He bought one – boasting a big Mick Jagger tongue looking like an American flag. But why? What was he thinking? Was he hoping that when the awful career-defining moment came, it might make him look a touch rebellious, saying: what do I care if I lose my job? Or more carefree and a touch younger, so worth keeping on..?

As he emerged into the frantic busy-ness of George Street, he threw the bad-news paper into the nearest bin. He wouldn't be taking it home for Fiona to read.

In the fateful event, he didn't wear the zany T-shirt, realising the Jagger image would make him look more ridiculous than rebellious. He was as crisp-collared as ever at his Market Street station when Monday's call came. Invited to "come in and pull up a chair, Roderick", he could barely hear the boss's fateful words spoken from the heavy jowels above an oddly empty desk; but the sonorous tones, spoken with a distinct air of *schadenfreude,* confirmed for Roddy that life as he knew it was about to end.

"I doubt if you'll be interested, but..." Indeed, a lesser shopfloor role was grudgingly offered. And the smidgen of pride Roddy still had left would not allow him to even consider it. Should he stick out his tongue in Jagger style and tell them where to stuff their consolation job? Maybe not. He wouldn't get much satisfaction in that as they'd probably already decided that's what they'd do with it. He forced out a weak smile, shook the flabby hand, accepted the consolation of a month's settlement salary without expectation of continued attendance, and took his head-down leave.

None of which would make the aspirational Fiona jump for joy. Indeed, he wouldn't be surprised if, on hearing the news, she left him in utter disgust. So if he wanted to keep his fragile marriage intact, which he did, she wouldn't hear the news...yet. It would be best she didn't know immediately. For a while anyhow, he'd refrain from being the shootable messenger. There would be that month's settlement salary to lean on in the meantime, not to mention the extra £2,000 from Angus's pipes. And was he really morally bound to send off half of it to that mystery bank number scribbled on his final note? Maybe one day, when things were going better...

It occurred that he was about to mislead his wife not just about his job, but on several fronts. By the simple withholding of information. But was that really so bad? His motive was honourable, he told himself – as he was just trying to spare her additional worries. In any case, he'd always reckoned crimes of omission were more acceptable than those of commission. And he certainly wouldn't be telling her in a hurry about the Elvis tribute act he was about to embark on (though the £60 fee would help bring home the bacon, or even the vegan alternative).

So come next Monday, Roddy would be a free man. Which sounded a lot better than it felt. But as far as Fiona would know, he'd be going back and forth to work every day as usual, for as long as it might take to find new employment.

He would try, in the meantime, to convince himself that impersonation too was in fact an honourable pursuit, bringing much-loved stars back to their fans. Practitioners often got a bad press for being copycats without originality, but he recalled a telling passage he'd read on that matter many moons ago: the wise words of the politically incorrect petrolhead Jeremy Clarkson.

* * *

When he got home, he found the book – *How Hard Can It Be?* – on a packed shelf of dusty volumes in the garage, and retrieved the pertinent passage within minutes:

When elderly people go to hear Rachmaninoff's Third, no-one is ever disappointed to find that it isn't actually the man himself on the ivories. Indeed, many derive a great deal of pleasure in hearing how other musicians interpret the great man's work. In fact, when you stop and think about it, the London Symphony Orchestra is a tribute band. It simply turns up and plays music written by someone else.

It had an emboldening effect. Two days later, with Fiona off to work again, he was back in the garage with a new courage – and an old dog. Which looked at him quizzically as he grappled the great white suit out of hiding from behind his gardening rags. Leg by flared leg, he climbed into it... to happily find it fitted like a glove, even round the big-buckled waist, even up to the high-collared neck.

He smiled into a cobwebbed old mirror leaning against the back wall. "Looks pretty good, eh Shep?" he said to the dog. "What d'you think?" Shep made a whining sound that sounded rather like disapproval. So Roddy would, in jest, return the sentiment...

He picked up the gift guitar he now regarded as his own, found a suitable starting chord, and let rip. "*You ain't nothin' but a hound dog!*" he blasted at the confused canine. Who now started to howl like a distressed wolf.

Together they made a huge noise that couldn't be missed across the street. And as they re-emerged under the up-swinging garage door, he shouldn't have been surprised to see two open-mouthed passers-by staring over the privet hedge.

"Christ, it's Elvis," said a corpulent boiler-suited man who looked like a plumber.

"Don't be daft," said an old shopping-bagged lady beside him. "Elvis has thick black hair, and he doesn't have a beard." She added with matter-of-fact disdain: "He certainly isn't ginger."

Did she think he certainly wasn't dead either? That wouldn't surprise him. From what he had heard and read lately about tribute acts, it seemed that, to some, the passing of the originals was a mere irritating detail. But...

Slinking wordlessly back into the house with Shep at his cowboy-booted heels, Roddy knew what he had to do now.

Kiss the beard goodbye and...

Despite being an eye-catching blonde, on special occasions Fiona had occasionally plumped to be a black-haired Cher lookalike. He would now have to find her wig.

That would complete the look with which to wow the golden oldies with his golden oldies.

Chapter 8

Call yourself a singer...

He hadn't realised it. He knew she was clever, with too many brains for her own good, but surely he would have noticed in eighteen years of living together. That Fiona had a big head; bigger than his anyway. He'd found her jetblack Cher wig in her dressing table, under a pile of knickers, in an aptly named (he joked to himself) bottom drawer. But it didn't really fit him, sliding about a little on his too-red head. It wasn't all bad, though. As he sat to adjust it in front of the table's big mirror, giving the occasional Elvis grunt, he thought the impression was pretty good. Especially when he added a curled top lip and a pair of shades. But...

There were no breaks in the sides of the hairpiece. Short of growing them with his own hair and dyeing the result, how could he make those famous sideburns stand out? He would have to cut gaps into each side of the false hair. Of course she would be furious, apoplectic, if she ever found out. But she wouldn't, would she? She hadn't worn the thing for years. And after his years as a medic, cutting bloody shirts from damaged people, he was quite handy with a pair of scissors.

So he went ahead, clipping away until the desired effect was achieved. Almost. Only the beard remained in the way, so he took up the scissors again and went for it. A few razor strokes saw it was no more. Then he found himself looking with satisfaction into the hazel eyes of an astonishingly near thing to Elvis... the black-haired, heavily-sideburned King.

"Now there's only the small matter of The Voice to be dealt with," he mused.

For that, it was back to the little garage again. With the dog again. Who would gradually stop howling, resurrecting the siren soundtracks of his tough old ambulance days.

Ah, soundtracks! After three days practising with a dozen Presley recordings, then with karaoke tracks from his phone, he felt he'd got most of the unique Elvis inflections and was ready as he'd ever be. Not with the guitar, of course; it would take another couple of years to get all the chords right on that, and if he was honest to himself, he found it too tricky to sing and play well at the same time. Anyway, although he could play it, Elvis had tended only to use his guitar as a prop.

Roddy knew, however, that relying on his cellphone for backing wasn't going to work in the long run, if he was to make a real fist of this exercise. He'd have to get some kind of speaker system. But meanwhile, for the old folks, the impression would surely be pretty acceptable, he allowed himself.

In the event, at his first appearance, not everyone agreed. They were gathered in a big hall-like room with high windows that gave the feeling of being deep in the woods. There were about forty of them cackling around him in a semi-circle, some sitting upright, some slumped a bit, others flat on trolleys and a few in wheelchairs. No one looked younger than eighty, so they couldn't be music critics of the highest order. Could they?

Sitting on a high bar stool as Elvis in all his glory, Roddy got his first karaoke track ready to roll, coughed a little and said in (what he thought was) a perfect Memphis accent: "How ya doin' folks? Ah just wanna sing you a little song. How about *Heartbreak Hotel*? Dunno 'bout you but it's one o' ma all-time favourites."

There was a little smattering of weak applause then a shaky but sharp female voice rose above it. "Ah dinnae like that one," it said.

"Well, baby, how about *Blue Suede Shoes*?" Still in his Elvis accent.

"Ah dinnae like that one either," came back the voice... owned, he noted, by a beanie-hatted lady with a wheelchair but with no teeth who was obviously a troublesome inmate with a condition.

"How about *Living Doll*?" she challenged him.

"Sorry, I don't do Cliff Richard. I'm supposed to be Elvis." The accent was slipping, as he ran his hands over his suit as if to illustrate his point. "Anyway, I don't know the words."

"Whit?!" countered the old lady. "Call yourself a fuckin' singer and ye don't know the fuckin' words to *Living Doll*?"

He badly wanted to return the F-word compliment in his own basic accent, but this gig was too important to mess up with bad blood. So to keep a lid on things, he said: "I'll try it then." As she was wheeled away by a nurse, he sang out the few words he knew of that number … *Got myself a cryin', talkin', sleepin', walkin', livin' doll… Fading, fading, fading, u*ntil a blessed, if awkward, silence enveloped everyone.

When a little hubbub returned, he tried again, nervously laughing off his first introduction, then repeating it; then changing it a little, with: "Ah feel like somebody just stood on ma toes. So Ah'll give you due warnin', folks, about ma blue suede shoes."

He'd barely rattled out *"One for the money, two for the show, three to get ready, then go cat go..."* when the place was enveloped in something quite different from that cold interruption; not warmth exactly, more like heat. The old folks hadn't forgotten the magic of Elvis's arrival on the world stage more than six decades earlier and, with arms waving in time, they rocked from side to side, in something like nostalgic ecstasy. The joint was jumping, as were the arthritic joints. If they could have, they would have stood up and danced.

One did, in fact, try. She swayed over to him, almost falling over, but managed to stretch a wrinkled hand out to caress his head. At which point, the wig shifted and, had it not been for his shades, would have fallen over his eyes. That lady, too, was led away, while the rest of the audience seemed to think it was funny.

He laughed too; then, responding with growing confidence, served up some of the ex-truck driver's best-known hits one after the other – *Heartbreak Hotel, The Girl of My Best Friend, Lawdy Miss Clawdy, Are You Lonesome Tonight?* He finished with a reference to the "cruel" comments that had blotted the start of his show. To which he offered *Don't Be Cruel* as a closing musical response. When it was done, he swung off the guitar, bowed, grabbed his head, said "Thank you so much, folks" and walked off to what seemed to him like a deafening applause.

"God, what are they on?" he said breathlessly to the waiting Elsie, as he adusted the wig again, that bow having introduced gravity to the proceedings.

"Mainly pork pie and chips," she said.

"Sorry about the start-up problem," he said, patting the

pate finally into place. "And the slipping hairpiece. Was it okay otherwise?"

"Okay? Are you kidding? It was fabulous. They loved you. So we'll definitely have you back again. And again. Maybe even once a week."

He smiled with deep relief then wondered about the several items she was clutching with both hands. "What have you there?" he asked, still breathless.

She lifted her mobile phone and showed him some of his act that she'd filmed. He looked on and chuckled, especially at the Cliff section.

"This is no joke," she said. "If you want to pursue this as a secondary career, you'll need to do something about the hair." She ruffled his carrot top a little. "And you'll need my little video as a demo. I'll ping it to you tonight, and to U Tube."

"Yeah, okay, so who should *I* send it to?" Roderick, with nothing left to lose, was sceptical but open enough to opportunities just to go along with it.

"Try this," she said, handing him a business card. "We've had dealings with him when in need of bigger performers for bigger productions. Did us proud a couple of Christmases ago."

The card bore the logo for GLK Promotions and a Falkirk address, followed by the name Ken Maybury. "Because if anyone bites you'll also need an agent or a promoter. I know this guy has at least one Elvis act on his books. But who knows, maybe he'd go for another as good as you."

"Well, thank-you, Mama," he said, pocketing the card. "How kind! But what else are you hiding there?" he said, noting her still-folded hands.

"Money," she said with a smile. And there it was, nestling in her open palm. His first earnings as an Elvis tribute act! Three £20 polymer Clydesdale Bank notes. Bearing the face of

Robert the Bruce, another famous king, the Elvis of Scotland's 14th century. He smiled back with unalloyed sincerity as he took them and put them in the same pocket.

"I could get used to this," he said.

"How was work today?" asked Fiona when their paths crossed briefly in the early morning, post-night-shift bed. What could he say? He was pretty sleepy but he could still invent a response that wasn't entirely dishonest.

"A bit rocky," he said, then turned over to go back to sleep.

But she wouldn't let him. Not yet. She peered closer into his face, which was usually covered when she went to bed. They'd just been passing ships in the last few nights. But what was this? A bare chin showing above the duvet? "Your beard has disappeared," she almost shouted. "Why on earth did you shave it off?"

"I just wanted to be like Elvis," he said, again finding honesty a good policy for deceit.

"That'll be the day," she scoffed.

"No, that's Buddy," he grunted. "Buddy Holly."

They both laughed a little and retired into Dreamland.

Chapter 9

Elvis, meet Elvis

"You gotta get a leg going," said the man from GLK Promotions, having pointed out that he was not an agent; that he was, in fact, a promoter of tribute acts (if they were good enough) "but also a comedy hypnotist".

Roddy wasn't meeting him in person, so couldn't figure whether he worked out of a high-end office or his kitchen table; but he seemed like a pro-active guy who could get stuff done. Indeed, he had just been the prime mover behind a spectacular *Absolute Elvis* show at the Glasgow's SSEC.

Big snag regarding that: there was already, as Elsie had suggested, a great would-be Elvis on his books. One Johnny Lee Memphis, star of that show which had pulled in "a wildly enthusiastic audience of three thousand", and who surely wouldn't welcome sharing the books with such an amateur interloper. So the question was: Would the name on the business card – Ken Maybury – see Roddy as a workable project in view of this inconvenient fact, and also of his raw amateur status?

But the man, having studied Elsie's little video, repeated his advice on the phone: "You gotta get a leg going."

"What do you mean?"

"What do you mean what do I mean? Don't you speak English? Come to think of it, neither do I. We'll try Scottish then. Shoogle it. You've got to shoogle if you want to be on Google."

"I get it."

"Good, it'll help get the ladies interested."

"I'm a happ...I'm a married man."

"All I'm saying is: use your noodle and shoogle if you want to be on Google."

"God, are you a poet as well?"

"Don't call me God. Ken will do. And yes, I'm a poet too. Jack of all trades, master of none."

"I know that feeling," said Roddy with feeling. Then all he could add was: "Which leg, Ken?"

"Doesn't matter. Just one of the two. Getting a leg going gets the girls going."

"Girls? You mean middle-aged ladies and beyond, surely. Their hero would have been in his eighties by now, so the legs might have been a touch over-shoogly. And his fans will be getting on a bit too, I imagine!"

"Well, maybe. But you'd be surprised how incredibly... er, lively they can be. Not to mention their granddaughters."

Why were they talking like this? It occurred to Roddy that the very existence of this rather silly conversation might mean there was some interest there, which must have been prompted by nothing more than Elsie's shaky movie.

Up to now, there had been only two more gigs at The Haven, three sessions at a couple of dog-friendly pubs where Shep's howling to *Hound Dog* seemed to go down at least as well as Roddy's singing; and a failed try-out at the Hard Rock Cafe which hadn't been happy with his (lack of a) sophisticated sound system. Which was why he now found himself at the Richer Sounds electronics store in Chambers Street, responding to its promise of "sound" advice on speakers and video and loop systems.

He hadn't been expecting such a call and, ironically, had to step outside the sound shop to improve the sound of it.

"We should meet," said Ken. "Where are you?"

"Edinburgh, at the famous speakers corner."

"Take my advice: hold off on speakers for the moment. I might have a better idea. But as I say, we should meet first. I should see you in action. Maybe kill both these birds with one stone?

"So where are you... Glasgow?"

"Malaga."

"Oh, I can't..." He was about to say he couldn't afford the fare, but Ken got in first.

"Don't worry. I'm just on a short break after the *Absolute Elvis* left me absolutely Elvised out. I'll be back in Scotland in a couple of days. In fact, we'll be in Edinburgh, me and Johnny Lee, in two weeks. He's performing at the Churchill Theatre. Just come along and we'll get you up for a guest spot. One number on stage. No need to costume up for it. I know how you look in it, I know how you can sing; I just need to know how you move. Wasn't much of that on your demo. And for the rest of the evening we'll get good seats for you and the wife."

"Oh, she's a nurse, sure to be on a late shift that night. She's not much of an Elvis fan either. So I don't think she'd be interested in coming. But my dog would."

"Your dog? Is that necessary?" The natural good cheer in Ken's voice turned to alarm.

Roddy realised he might be trying to combine a career move with a dog-sitting problem. "No, of course not. I'll arrange for him to be looked after. It's just that he usually comes along with me when the wife's at work."

"Really?"

"He can be quite funny actually."

"Really? How so?"

"When I sing *Hound Dog*, he howls like a wolf, trying to join in, I suppose."

"Really?" There was a long pause in Malaga, then Ken said: "Bring the dog."

Ken seemed about to finish the exchange, but Roddy had to ask: "Why is it so important you see how I move?"

"You won't remember, but you may have heard how our great inspiration was dubbed Elvis the Pelvis in his early years?" Ken's underlying laughter was creeping back into his disembodied voice.

"Vaguely, I suppose. Because of how he moved, wasn't it?"

"Yeah! And I've thought of a great stage name for you in the same spirit. But if we get an act going it would depend on you keeping fit... moving and looking pretty damned good."

"What's the name then?"

"Don't laugh."

"I won't laugh. I promise. What is it?"

"Roddy the Body"

They both laughed their hearts out before hanging up.

Two weeks! So little time to check things out. Was he imagining it, or was he being considered as a professional "project"? Would he be gutted if he wasn't? If he was, would it make any financial sense? It would surely be much more fun, but could pretending to be Presley earn at least as much as the store job he'd left behind? "Superstar versus superstore!" he joked to himself.

But it really wasn't funny. Bearing Fiona's expected reaction in mind, he'd have to do some due diligence before Johnny Lee's show. Maybe he could talk to some established Scots practitioners? Get the real facts that came with the fantasy. Yes, he'd try to find a few...

A few minutes' online searching turned up dozens in the UK – was the Elvis industry replacing the car industry? – but only a few were connected to Scotland. Paul Thorpe, an Englishman based in Falkirk, was up for coffee near his home – though Rob Kingsley, creator of the *Vision of Elvis* show, and an Edinburgh-born Scot based in England, could manage only a phone call. Then there was "co-star" Johnny Lee Memphis, whom he'd soon meet anyway, though maybe a preparatory heads-together would make sense. So he called, to be told by an open, friendly voice: "Sure, Roddy, let's do it." Coffee was arranged for a week before "their" show.

All the tribute artists had rich tales of how they got into the "industry" and what they were getting out of it... which included money, though they seemed to so enjoy the game he could imagine them doing it for charity. Just as that crossed his mind, a related news item popped across his screen. It said: *The Rev Wynne Roberts, a hospital chaplain who has raised £250,000 for charity by performing as Elvis, has been rewarded with the British Empire Medal. The 58-year-old from Anglesey performs up to 100 shows a year to raise money for various causes and sings for folk in care homes, particularly those with dementia. He said: "When you sing as the King the negative effect of that illness is taken away from people."*

So there was enough money in it even to give away hundreds of thousands! And there was obviously no age limit, no dictated retirement age. Blimey, this man was nearly 60, going strong nearly twenty years over the age (42) that saw the original bite the dust. What was it Johnny Carson said about this? "If life was fair, Elvis would be alive and all the impersonators would be dead." So how old were the Scots would-be Elvi that Roddy felt he could identify with? Turned out Paul was 54, for instance, and Johnny Lee 44.

Roddy realised that, if he managed to join them in representing Scotland, he'd be the youngest by a country mile. So what advice would these veterans have for such a youngster?

Rob's career success suggested that, if he got going, he ought not to limit himself to gigs north of the Border; there were many, many places all over the UK – and beyond – that would never lose their insatiable appetite for Elvis. It seemed everybody wanted to see (and hear) the great man alive again, strutting the stage again; never having left the building.

Paul, a one-time dustman and bingo caller discovered on *Stars in Your Eyes* in 1993 before soon making £2,000 a week in Grand Canaria hotels, warned him: "The women! It's unreal. Beware of the adoration!"

"But tribute acts could never be the real thing for these Elvis-lovers," suggested Roddy.

"To them, you *are* the real thing," said Paul.

And when they met near JLM's modest home in Tillicoultry, Clackmannanshire, Johnny Lee concurred: "Yes you are, it's scary. And you sometimes have to remind yourself who you are." Under his dark blue baseball cap, he was really John Fleming. Having fun-dressed as Elvis since childhood, he'd once had a mini identity crisis himself. Now cured of it, he was able to step easily from multi-award-winning Elvis, thrilling crowds of three thousand, to being a simple family man.

"But how did you get into it?" Roddy asked.

Turned out, he'd been in a local band anyway, so musical diversions with some Presley numbers were pretty regular. A one-time slater and latterly a gym instructor, he got nightly stage experience mainly as Elvis in Minorca, during a six-month sabbatical from Falkirk Council's employ. Halfway through the holiday, he decided to ditch the day job. "Well, my wife decided actually. It was her idea, based on simple maths. If I got £1,400 a month from the gym and £700 a show as Elvis, I only had to do two shows a month to make it work. So it was a pretty logical decision."

These days, of course, there were venue charges, band members and backing singers to pay from much bigger show revenues. But all things considered, it couldn't be denied that all the Elvis tribute artists he'd talked to were not only doing well financially, but – even more importantly – feeling pretty happy about life as well.

"What's in that backpack, if I might ask?" said Johnny Lee, pointing a big black North Face rucksack which Roddy had deposited on an adjacent seat when he sat down at their cafe table. It was beginning to make its presence felt.

"My Elvis outfit," replied the novice. "Or I should say, my late dad's Elvis outfit. I've no idea if it's the right thing... you know, quality-wise. No idea whether it's rubbish or the best there is, though it feels pretty good to me. Can you help?"

"Maybe I can," said Johnny with a laugh. "I've got twelve Elvis outfits at home, all top quality; the dearest one cost me £4300 and the cheapest £900. So I reckon I'd know a good one on sight."

Roddy unpacked the bag slowly and Johnny's eyes widened as the pure white creation made its full, magnificent appearance. Flared legs dripping with laces and golden buttons, then the big belt with a square buckle like the golden frame of an old master; then the jacket, embroidered in front like that of a matador, in the back with the dramatic Indian-style image of a golden eagle; then the high starched collar reminiscent of medieval kings.

"Phew," said Johnny cradling much of it against his knees and sniffing the wool jersey fabric like an expert. "It's been worn, but it's also been cleaned. Still very serviceable but I'd guess it's been hanging around for a good while."

"I reckon you'd be right there," said Roddy. "Hanging around...literally. Among the many other sartorial items in my old man's thoughtful legacy."

"Maybe more thoughtful than you thought! It's the real deal, I'd say, and how!"

"How?"

"I can tell the embroidery is by Gene Doucette, who fancied up most of the Elvis's suits after they were designed by Bill Belew. Elvis loved the embroiderer's work, but they never met...can you believe that? And this design is definitely by Belew. So you've got a winner here. I'd say it's worth at least four grand if you ever want to sell it."

"Wow," said Roddy. "Where would my dad have got the money to buy something like that?"

"Where indeed? But remember, he was once young and maybe even a babe magnet. Though it must have been a very early ETA moment."

"Estimated Time of Arrival?"

"Naw, I mean... did he perform as an Elvis Tribute Act.... ETA, as we insiders now know it?"

"I very much doubt it... the mind boggles at the thought."

"So why would your old man have got himself an Elvis suit then?"

"That's a good question," said Roddy. "A very good question."

Would he ever find the answer? Somehow, being on the cusp of new and adventurous discoveries, he felt he would. And in that learning spirit, he'd take all he could from Scotland's go-to Elviseer. "Anything I ought to know about the industry?" he asked. "Not least – how long has it got, with first-generation fans getting older and dying out?"

Johnny smiled cheekily. "They've said that for years... decades. But even if their grandparents fade away, the younger ones still revere the legend; so I find my audiences are actually growing. It's still cool to be a fan. I reckon there's at least ten or fifteen years of Elvis appreciation left, and it wouldn't surprise me if it went on for another forty or fifty. Bach still pulls in crowds doesn't he? "

"Any advice then?"

"How long have you got?"

Roddy's Americano grew cold as he supped the hot tips imparted by this star ETA who was fast becoming his mentor...

"But," he said, "don't copy other ETAs. Not even me! Take your lessons only from the master. Study his movements and sing along with him again and again with the best backing track; just you and him. Not just for the voice tones, also to perfect the diction and accent.

"That said, be true to yourself. When you're talking between songs, don't try to mimick the great man's recorded words, but get a feel for his personality and try to imagine what he'd have said in this or that situation.

"On stage, drink loads of water or pineapple juice to keep your voice in tune. Never alcohol, as that dries out the throat."

"Anything else?"

"Stay safe. Avoid unruly fans, and try to control the enthusiastic females in the nicest possible way without becoming... em... inappropriate."

"Thank you kindly," said Roddy, his grin turning to a grimace as he drained his cold coffee. "It's now or never!"

He couldn't wait for the Churchill Theatre show.

He was done with dreaming.

Roddy the Body was ready to rock.

Chapter 10

The Churchill show

"Hi, man!" Four dark-dressed players of two electric guitars, a keyboard, big drums, and two glittery female singers peered into the middle seats to witness the arrival of new man with dog. Only one of the girls actually speaking: "Welcome."

Roddy peered back. It wasn't just the sight of them that made his jaw drop but also their fabulous sounds – which would certainly beat looking up karaoke backing tracks on his iphone.

Was he really going to get professional backing like this just for one song? The four were known as the JLM band, after Johnny Lee Memphis, and the second lot, boasting full figures wrapped in high-glam dresses, were the Memphis Belles. "Hi," he replied, trying not to look overawed.

He was glad he hadn't gone for the full Elvis image, so as not to be presumptuous... not to annoy the real star; that he'd limited his outfit to a plain white T-shirt, jeans and Fiona's wig. Especially when Johnny himself appeared, warming up with them in the glare of under-test spotlights, as the crowds began to trickle into the old Churchill Theatre in the heart of Morningside. Reassuringly Elvis-like in sight and sound, and clutching an acoustic guitar, he wasn't yet in the full Doucette-Belew gear when he called Roddy and Shep up on to the boards...

"You both behave now please, while we sort out your key and stuff," he said with a smile, as he rubbed the dog's forehead. Shep responded with a busy wagging of his tail. Roddy fixed the key with the guitar men and, everyone being familiar with the song, there was no more delay. A sudden bang on the snare drum was the signal for them to barrel straight into a rehearsal of *Hound Dog* – with Johnny hanging back to give Roddy the main part, supported by his howling hound. Which meant that, while bursting into great, driving music, the band also burst into fits of laughter.

"Sorry, he's too loud," said a nervous Roddy to all concerned as the music stopped.

But they all clapped, smiled and let Johnny to speak for them. "No, no, he's great," he said. "The fans will love him. They like the show to be full of fun and humour." Shep gave a modest bark just to put a full point on the thought.

True to his word, when the *Absolute Elvis* show got properly underway, Johnny – now all white on the night – got quite a laugh on introducing himself in a deep southern drawl: "Well, hi...a very good evenin' to y'all, ladies and gennelmen. It's just kinda wunnerful to be here in Scadland...in Edinboro." Adding in local dialect: "Ah dinnae really speak like that; I'm frae Stirling."

For all that he didn't speak like the show's late legendary inspiration, he certainly sang like him, noted Roddy, imagining that they could have owned the same voice box. Every mood and move was authentically caught, from the rocking *I Got A Woman* through the mid-rhythm *What You Want Me To Do* to the slow and sensitive *One Night With You*.

Johnny's almost-shy relaxed way, and love of Presley songs sung with huge confidence, made Roddy a little less tense. And when, after eight numbers, he and Shep were called in from the wing to do their thing, he reckoned he could, with a chuckle, blame the dog if things went wrong.

As they almost stumbled on to centre stage to a big drum roll and pointed spotlights, there was some uncertain applause and some oohs and aahs obviously prompted by the dog's star quality.

"We've got a couple of handsome amateurs here for you tonight," said Johnny to the hundreds of mainly grey-haired heads in the darkness of the auditorium. "But we know talent when we see it. Or hear it, I should say. So we're giving local fellas Roddy and Shep their big chance right now, and we hope you'll give them a matching big hand for their unique version of *Hound Dog.*"

"Which one is which?" a male voice called from the stalls.

"This one is Roddy," said Johnny as he handed over the guitar. Roddy gratefully hoisted the prop around himself, and said "Wow" as he looked into the sea of expectant faces. Then to Shep: "Now you say bow!" No doggy response, so he added, with a small stoop: "I'll do the bow then." All of which got him off to a good-humoured start – ignited again by the snare drum's bang.

If the shaking of a leg was essential to the exercise, as Ken had urged, Roddy's nerves made sure there was no problem there. His right leg was bouncing up and down with involuntary energy like a hand-held road leveller, hugely aided by the band's driving beat. His voice seemed similarly possessed, inspired by his mentor's bold execution. Big, strong and uninhibited were the words that that performance brought to mind, and he'd go for them too.

It was heady stuff, and he didn't know if it was normal to be in a bit of haze, to get a wildly enthusiastic response from the fans. But the applause that seemed most sympathetic came from Johnny who joined the audience's appeal for an encore as he clapped. He even helped with a guitar backing when they all managed to squeeze an unrehearsed rendering of *Old Shep* out of the pair, with Shep the eponymous hero, again in full voice.

As dog and master retired with a bow – and a bow-wow – Roddy had virtually no recollection of their performance. All he could recall was the hovering presence of promoter Ken, circling him with a big movie-making tablet held at arm's length. Passing technicians assured him their appearance had been "just terrific", but he wasn't so sure.

He felt unable wait for the post-show verdicts of his fellow performers; so sure was he that some opinions would be devastatingly negative. Not least because of the canine gimmickry. So he missed the last few numbers and snuck out through the empty foyer and allowed Shep to relieve himself in the gutter of a nearby pavement.

"That was a piece of shit," he said, before allowing himself to hail a taxi.

Meanwhile, the show rattled on, as Johnny Lee Memphis and the Memphis Belles swept through a second half bulging with some of the King's greatest hits – like *All Shook Up, Burnin' Love, Lawdy Miss Clawdy, Just Can't Help Believin', Can't Stop Loving You, Don't Be Cruel, Johnny B. Goode, Suspicious Minds,* and a memorable American Trilogy featuring *Dixieland*, *Glory Glory*, and *All My Trials*. As he wrapped himself in a huge Stars and Stripes.

What Roddy also missed was Johnny's philosophical conclusion – a spoken–not–sung reminder to himself and others about the identity risks of being a great pretender.

"Remember, there can only ever be one Elvis. All we can do is be the best kind of tribute band we can be and never forget the great man for his great music."

Chapter 11

An unrefusable offer

On morning-after reflection, if decibel level was anything to go by, his guest spot at the Churchill had maybe been a success. The waved phones, applause and excited kerfuffle had also excited Old Shep who had raised his leg and let loose at *Hound Dog*'s concluding moment. Roddy hoped no one had noticed.

But had the shaking of *his* leg been noticed? How much of his inimitable shoogle had fanned the fans' fever? If any. How much had been down to his vocal grip on the material?

He knew he owed much of the noisy reaction to other voices – of the original Pelvis and one handsome hound with a howl. And he knew that eventually, if he was to become a name doing justice to the portrait beside his boots, he'd have to drop the prop. He could already hear Ken saying: "Time to drop the hot dog, my friend. He was great, but..."

Then Roddy the Body would be on his own.

It was now the morning after. Still throbbing from that surreal theatrical experience, he'd driven eighty miles – in what felt like a religious pilgrimage in search of reassurance – down to Scotland's south-west just to walk where his Great Inspiration once walked. Sixty years before. And now he was looking down at the four-tile-square plaque in the floor of Prestwick airport's foyer and trying *not* to walk on the yellow star with central image of his hero framed in black. Under the main heading of the great man's name were the words:

Prestwick is the only place in the United Kingdom visited by the King of Rock 'n' Roll. Sergeant Presley was greeted by screaming fans on 3 March, 1960, when his aircraft stopped to refuel.

He wondered why the caption didn't explain that the serving soldier had been flying from his base in Germany on his way back to the US… and why, in view of the airport's six decades of celebrating that magical moment, it had not renamed itself Presley Airport. It seemed close enough to work pretty well. But maybe the management was still inhibited by the sergeant's memorable words on alighting from the plane: "Where am I?"

"Where are you?" were the first words Ken the Promoter spoke when Roddy answered his phone.

"Prestwick airport. Which should really be called Presley airport."

"Why are you there?"

"Just feeling the great man's leftover vibes."

"Ok. I get it. We missed you last night after the show. We all wanted to talk but you'd gone."

"I had to get my dog to bed. He was kinda tired and over-excited; had already disgraced himself. Didn't you see it? Who's 'we all'?"

"Johnny Lee… the JLM band guys… the Memphis Belles… me."

"I suppose y'all wanted to advise me to forget it." Roddy's imposter syndrome had already kicked in. An imposter as an impersonator, that was quite rich.

"On the contrary, Roddy. We thought your number was fabulous. Great look. Great singing. Johnny Lee was specially impressed."

"Why would he be? I'm an interloper who could step on his toes ...shoes even."

"Blue suede ones even."

They both laughed a little and another voice broke in. Johnny Lee himself, speaking in a warm Scottish brogue, as the original John Fleming, one-time slater and plasterer. "The fact is, Roddy, we've got too much work on and I can't spread myself so much. I have an interest in the business and there's only one Johnny Lee Memphis on the books. Fact is, we need at least a second Elvis. But he has to be good enough."

"And you guys think I'm good enough?"

Ken again: "We do."

Roddy gave out an audible "Phew" and wiped some sweat beads from his forehead, causing the black eyebrow pencil that had darkened his sandy brows last night to smear across his cheeks.

Johnny echoed: "We do. We've seen enough to know you're worth working on. Maybe a couple of points need tweaking. Some voice nuances and presentation; keeping that body in ...er...desirable shape; and stuff like your facial make-up. I spend forty minutes on that every show. So I'll give some advice on that in the next weeks. To get you oven-ready, as Boris might say.

"Then maybe you can start to think bigger. Forget your wee speaker problems for a start. We'll be talking big bands, several backing singers and speakers to blow your ears out."

Ken: "And money to blow your eyes out."

Roddy: "Really?"

Ken: "Yeah, man! We don't think small here. Johnny has performed across the world – China, Canada, Norway, Australia, Italy, Spain, Spain, Sweden ...not to mention the good old US of A. You name it, he's done it. Even sung for the Queen as part of her Jubilee party in Glasgow."

Roddy realised he needed a drink. He saw a sign for the airport's Graceland Bar and, still holding his phone to his ear, made his way across the concourse towards it. Had Elvis also walked this way? There were ghostly images related to him all over the place. It was all getting too exciting. "What kind of money? Can I ask?"

"We could be talking £800 per show," said Ken, "and an average of maybe five shows a month. Often with a percentage of the profits. We can guarantee you won't be feeling under the weather financially ever again. If you take us on."

Roddy sat down at a bar stool and ordered a beer. He wasn't going to overdo it. He had Shep waiting in the car and still had to drive him home safely. "So *you* want to take *me* on? Is that what you're saying?" His heart leapt as they both replied in unison: "Absolutely, Elvis."

"Where have I heard that before?" chuckled Ken, adding: "But just one more thing..."

"I think I know what you're gonna say," said Roddy.

"Yeah? What?"

"It's time to drop the hot dog. He was great, but..."

"Yeah. That's exactly what I was gonna say. How did you know?"

"Dunno, must be psychic," Roddy said, half-spluttering into the last of his beer. But there was one wee point to be clarified. "Would there be something in writing then?"

"Sure," said Ken. "There'll be something in the post. Confirming our interest. Writing you into the books as one of our Elvi. But not specifying regular income levels. This is still the gig economy we're talking about! But very apt for a musician, no?"

"Ok, any way you want me," said Roddy with a shrug, realising he had just quoted the name of a Presley song half-remembered from his garage rehearsals. He sang it shakily in the car as he made his way home, and Shep joined in, unaware that his rising star was already dimming. "Sorry, pal," Roddy said between verses, patting his eager head. "No hard feelings? It's cos you ain't nothin' but a hound dog."

Was there no end to the appetite for the cool young man who, had he lived, would now be in his eighties? The Elvis industry was really booming. As Roddy drove back into the capital, he couldn't miss the posters. Plastered on walls everywhere – announcing a great triple-Elvis show coming to town in a couple of weeks. Straight from America. "Kingsize Elvis!" the headline said, above the subhead "World tribute tour". Backed up by three handsome lookalikes in action; former tribute contest champions – Cooper Cross, Sean Cody and Krish Ray. He'd surely get tickets as these guys would be only two nights at The Playhouse. He'd doubtless learn some stuff from them too. They'd been getting rave reviews all over the world.

He might even take Fiona along to get her into the mood, before…

Before what? He gulped with sheer apprehension. Before… er…finally telling her that her beloved man had lost his proper job and was now being groomed as an Elvis tribute act to wow the world. Maybe.

He would have to pick the moment carefully.

Chapter 12

It's now or never

"Promises, promises!" he huffed at Shep as they tried to run off their anxieties along Portobello's "golden strand". That was the shouted promise of a nearby billboard, selling yet-to-be-realised joys of a new properties by the water's edge. Not quite so golden this morning, actually, with its snow blanket and not-so-jolly promenade stalls as cold as their summer ice cream. It had been nearly two weeks since he heard his world was to change for the bigger and better, but there had been precious little action.

Sure, Johnny Lee had urged him to fill his spare time with activity like this, had even come over twice to coach him and pass on tickets for the three-Elvis show "to learn from these guys". But so far, Roddy's own show career was anything but frenetic. Just a couple of care-home gigs. He was beginning to think he'd dreamed the Churchill triumph ...and the promoter's resulting "offer".

One of his many spare moments had been used to send

half the profit from his dad's bagpipes to the mysterious bank number found inside them. And that while his own cash worries mounted...

He and Fiona wouldn't manage much longer on unfulfilled promises; not that she knew of any. She knew only that his monthly "pay" kept coming in as normal, while the reality was anything but normal. Having missed the Morrisons bad-news item, she assumed Roddy's absence every noon, when she woke after a long night shift, was his store job just going on; when in fact they were living on her salary, his shrinking settlement, and the other half of the yield from Angus's pipes.

The last two of which were finite.

One way or another, whatever the near future held, he knew his wife must soon learn the truth. He'd just been hoping for a lifeboat to appear first, he thought, as he scanned the misted-up Forth horizon. But it was simply too slow in arriving.

"I'll speak to her tomorrow," he told the dog, who jumped up at his bare knees in apparent agreement before losing sight of him in a blast of freezing snowflakes.

The moment would still have to be carefully picked.

"Why the hell would I want to do that, Roderick?" was Fiona's reaction to his invite to join the big-show audience. "When would I find a moment when I work all the overtime God sends? I'm no Elvis fan anyhow. Something a wee bit more civilised – like a baroque ensemble or something – might just get me interested."

This hadn't started well, he noted, as his usually well-groomed wife sat up in bed and rubbed her fingers angrily through sleep-messed blonde hair. The hot-tea peace offering he'd brought her was just sitting there on the bedside table, ignored and getting cold. He knew the feeling.

"I thought you could do with a night out." Roddy sat down on the other side of the bed, showing her the tickets. "It's something different."

"Also..." She pushed forward with a start that made him recoil. "Where did you get the money to buy two expensive tickets like that?"

It wasn't lying to say: "They were given to me."

"Why? Why would any old someone just give you two tickets for a ....what is it...?" She almost snatched them from him and sneered as she read: "Kingsize Elvis concert featuring three world-famous tribute acts? Bloody hell."

This was his now-or-never moment. The chance to confess all. To reveal that he too might be entering that trade. But lucratively (maybe), to compensate for the lost day job. He began: "Because I ..." but couldn't finish; couldn't blurt out the awful truth. So this was, in fact, a moment to tell a shameful untruth. "Because I won them in a sales competition at work. Record figures last month."

She humphed, snuggled back down into her duvet, and dismissed him with a muffled "Let the dog out for a pee please".

"I take it that's a no then," he said, probably to himself, as he went to release the animal through the back door from the kitchen.

Shep chose his usual spot, melting ice to yellow on the crazy paving, but he might as well have pissed on his master. Roddy knew where he'd rather be right now. It was the day before the big concert. The three lucky Elvi would be in town now, rehearsing with their fabulous five-strong band and four sexy backing singers, enjoying it all and laughing even at their occasional slip-ups. How did he imagine that? Such professionals didn't make mistakes ...did they?

* * *

The drummer put all his energy into a long roll, the brass blew a fanfare fit for a king. A spotlight cut through the muted general lighting to focus on the figure high above the stage. "And now," called out Sam, the American compere, on a mic his hollering voice didn't need, "we present the final phase of the greatest entertainer the world has ever known!" The three ages of the King were here personified: Cooper as the young guy in jeans, Sean playing the established performer in full leather outfit; and Krish the matador-suited Las Vegas concert star. Cooper and Sean had done their practice stints and were now leaning back on their guitars, ready to applaud, representing the audience to be wowed by this scene tomorrow night.

It was a tense moment. There had been long arguments, on the tour bus and even here on the boards, about the merits of this aerial stunt idea – a "first" conceived by management across the pond. No-one denied it was risky, having Krish fly in from above like a bespangled angel, but the theatre's ropeworks had been thoroughly tested and only human practice was needed now. A cheeky voice, one of the English female backing singers, piped up: "I hope you're insured for this!" but the big-voiced Sam just laughed and called out "Now!"

As a big-wave surfer, bungee jumper and ex-fighter in Afghanistan, Krish himself was up for it… literally. He'd always been okay with risk. A flash of fear crossed his eyes as the order came, and it was the expected cheating of it he loved. Which was not to be in this case. He pulled in a deep breath and took off into the climaxing fanfare; as he fell, his flared pants filled up with air like mini-parachutes but not enough to brake his descent. The floor kept coming up too fast. With arms flailing, he crashed into it with a huge painful clatter, shattering more than his ego, and vaguely realising, before he passed out, that the rope had been a touch too long.

Less exciting at this point was Roddy's in-limbo life. With Fiona's reaction to his invite ringing in his ears, he gathered a big Canadian jacket over his Hard Rock Cafe T-shirt and left the whining dog with her. Setting out on slippery foot to get more exercise and rock-star vibes. It was the kind of thing actors did to get into a part, wasn't it? So: another coffee at that rocking cafe with music to throb to; it had to be an Americano, he being so into Americana these days. Then a longish walk past Murrayfield Stadium to Labinjoh's exotic old-car lot where, yes, among the Alfas and Porches and MGs he spied a cool pink 1950s Cadillac. Elvis's favourite winged monster! He chuckled as he imagined bringing it home to (fail to) fit in their little suburban driveway and garage. What a magnificent embarrassment that would be!

Then, of course, there was The Playhouse. Perhaps, if he passed nearby, he could hear some of the big-show rehearsal sounds. "I wonder…" he said to himself; words that insinuated a song into his head, so that he began quietly singing it, slightly adapted, *The Wonder of You*. It was steadily strangled by the hee-hawing of a white emergency vehicle sweeping past him. As he approached the theatre there was nothing more to hear. But there *was* something of a scene. With its blue lights still flashing, the ambulance was parked right in front of the main glass-panelled entrance. Obviously awaiting or about to help a customer.

"Someone slip on the ice?" Roddy asked through its wound-down front window, thinking he might know the driver from Back Then; but they were unknown to each other – and the medic's message was clear: rubber-necking passers-by were unwelcome in the face of action. The reply was a silent, negative shake of the head. In a way, Roddy understood that from his own experience, so he walked on while still, nevertheless, wondering.

Turning into London Road, the first bus stop with a few

brave souls gathered about it, seemed to offer some consolation. Speaking for his deep-frozen self, he'd had enough of being a brave soul. After three hours on his numbed feet, retreat was the order of the day. Retreat to the cosiness of home only a No 26 bus ride away. He sighed with relief. Or was it resignation? Or was it rejection? He wasn't to know it now, but under different circumstances, his deft touch with clothes-cutting scissors might have come in handy in the ambulance...

Krish was conscious and groaning when the stretcher-bearers hustled up to the stage and pushed through the circle of anxious co-stars – Cooper and Sean, their backing band members and singing girls. Plus Sam, compere and dynamic leader of the pack who, even before the medics could assess the damage, asked urgently: "Is he gonna be okay?" Another question that got a silent, shrugged response. But he soon saw for himself that Krish was not going to be okay. One clue was in the screaming, as he was manhandled on to the stretcher. Others were starkly visible. Though not yet cut free from his jumpsuit, it was plain his left leg was seriously out of order, with its knee where its thigh should have been. The screaming continued as he was hoisted into the ambulance; even as the flared pants were scissored into, all the way up to his now-immobile Elvis pelvis; and it didn't stop until the laughing gas began to work .

Krish was, understandably, too diverted to see the shock on his showmates' faces as they circled round to see him being driven off slowly to the Royal Infirmary. Most horrified of all was Sam, who jumped aboard with his suddenly disabled star. How bad could this be? He had to find out, pronto. And soon enough, he learned it was... "pretty bad". The medical conclusion, after a swift X-ray, was that Krish had a dislocated knee with the leg broken in two places. He'd have to be operated on for four hours to insert a plate and five screws; then kept in hospital for three or four days; then...

Sam tried to give his star nice, lying reassurances – "Don' t worry about nothin' buddy… you're gonna be fine" – but representing as he did the US tour promoters, he was seriously alarmed when Krish gave back only a groan; a noise echoed by the little dynamo when the doctors' final verdict came: "Your man won't be fit to perform or even walk – or fly – for up to twelve weeks." Sam gulped and spilled his weak NHS tea over himself with the receipt of such a stunning truth, and heard himself hollering "No, no, gaddamn it, no!" before being gently shown to a quiet room. Both he and Krish were decidedly, in the immortal words of their benefactor, All Shook Up.

Chapter 13

An unrefusable offer (2)

A blonde head popped in to find Sam red of face with phone clamped to his ear. He barely noticed the not-quite-senior nurse asking: "Will you be staying long to be with your friend, sir? I'm afraid he's not conscious yet and we'll soon need this room for him. But I can bring you a nice sandwich."

Often compared to Danny DeVito because of his small roundness and Big Apple twang, Sam Fantoni was not used to failure. Under his dark-blue New York Yankees baseball cap was a red velvet suit, open-necked denim shirt, white-laced boots and a tough character that would not be easily beaten by this. But he knew he was on the edge of panic. He signalled OK to the nurse with a nod and kept talking. As she closed the door, she heard him say: "Ain't no time to find a top guy, probably in England. Probably booked up anyhow. So what we gonna do? Wipe the whole fucking tour?"

"Find somebody local. On the goddamn doorstep."

"Somebody local? Jesus, that's a challenge!"

The US promotion company EL Vizz International had barely got into its morning stride when presented with this dilemma. It was 4.15pm in Edinburgh, 11.15am in New York... where dynamic decisiveness was a way of life. Indeed, it was the boss's PA who took Sam's call and felt she could make her own call. From twenty storeys high in a skyscraper, looking up to the Chrysler building. "You'll find one," insisted Cathy Ryder. "Shit, they're everywhere. Like a plague of goddamn locusts. Just train him up fast."

"And what if they...he...ain't good enough?"

"Reckon you just gotta come clean with the fans. Admit it... OK, we gotta problem here but YOU guys came up with the solution in your amazingly talented Whatever-his-name-is."

"Like who then, in God's name?"

"Let me refer to the Google god." A pause, then: "How about this Scotland-based Johnny Lee Memphis guy? He's won a whole lotta Elvis contests, even here in the States. Make them Scots feel proud we're celebrating their guy."

"Even if he's free, that ain't no permanent solution. In any case, think about it. If he's so well known here as a native talent, we can kiss goodbye to our all-American mystique. We need somebody who's kinda new to the audience, local or not."

"Yeah, in an ideal world maybe. But this is not ideal world. I reckon the Johnny Whatever guy..."

"Memphis. Johnny Lee Memphis."

"Will be a safe bet for now. Sorry, I got JJ's lunch to organise. I'll brief him on this, but I reckon he'll agree." She sounded so sure of her ground, Sam wondered about her sexual grip on her boss,. "If the guy is good, keep him on for the tour. We'll make a quick contract deal."

"He could be booked out."

"Just try it."

Sam sighed, then retook the air to present the next poser. "One more thing."

"Yeah? Make it quick."

"What do we do about Krish? He can't walk or even fly. For maybe even twelve weeks. That's more than the whole tour. Do we put him up in a hotel or what? He's already gonna cost us full salary."

"Half salary."

"And medical expenses before we hit the insurers on this."

"Sorry, no hotel for a time period like that, Sam. I can sure speak for management on that one. Byeee…"

As the nurse re-entered his little room, Sam threw his phone with one hand on to its single bed, and accepted the proffered sandwich with the other. "Thanks," he said absent-mindedly. "What's in it?" He was sure it would be, in good old American phraseology, good old British garbage.

"Cheese," she said. "Hard cheese."

"You can say that again," he said, biting into it with anger flashing across his little black eyes.

When he finished the so-called sandwich, he picked up the phone again, googled the name listed as Johnny Lee Memphis's representative, and called him: "Is that Ken Maybury?"

"The very one," came the breezy reply.

"Sam Fantoni here."

"I know of you. The big Elvis tour. In the big city this week. How can I help?"

"We've lost our third Elvis. Broken leg. To put it kinda bluntly, we need another. Here and now and fast. The show must go on tomorrow night. And the next night. We have in mind your Johnny Lee Memphis. Is he available?" Sam noticed that the stubby fingers of his left hand were crossed. As were his stubby legs; though that could have been his requirement for another kind of John.

"Sorry, he's extremely unavailable. Booked for four weeks on a cruise, as of this afternoon. Nice work if you can get it... eh?"

"Shit."

"Pardon?"

"Got anybody else?"

A four-second pause was followed by a slow, careful "Well, yeah, maybe I might..."

"Who?"

"He's new, a bit raw, but damned good, I'd say."

"You would say that, though, wouldn't you? What's the name?"

"Roderick Kirkwood. Or Roddy for short. Or Roddy the Body if you like."

Ken laughed again at his own rhyming inspiration, but Sam was too intensely focused to even smile. "How can I see what he's like?"

"I just happen to have a wee video." Ken's filming of the Churchill gig might be paying off already. "Not in Elvis gear, though he does possess a good white Belew jumpsuit. I'll ping you the movie now if you like."

"I like. Do that. Right now."

Ten minutes later, the Maybury phone in Falkirk rang again. "Hi, it's Sam."

"You got it? What d'you think?"

"Send the guy over to Edinburgh right now."

"He lives in Edinburgh."

"Great! The Playhouse Theatre. Within the hour. We'll be waiting. To try him at a short try-out rehearsal tonight before we sign him up ...probably. Then serious rehearsals tomorrow morning."

"Ok, but you gotta sign me up too. I don't do this stuff for fun."

"Anything you say. Send me your terms."

Sam's mood suddenly lifted. He caught a cab into town without having had a chance to comfort his unconscious post-op pal. But he felt the day might just have been saved. It was still only 5.30pm. With luck, he could steady the ship with a new, somewhat practised crew member by 8pm and get back to a revived Krish before his lights-out.

The telly was droning on but Roddy didn't hear a word of it. Lying back soporifically with Shep's head on his lap, he was glad just to be reheated, watching snow falling outside, and reading...the *Weekend Times* Fiona had left on the sofa's arm. As his eye scanned casually through it, a piece by Ashley Davies caught his interest. Headed *Everything you need to know about tribute bands*, it started with some observations worth bearing in mind...

Tribute bands are a bit like rebound relationships. No one believes they measure up to the original but they often have a better attitude and if you blur your eyes they can feel real enough.

As big-name bands become less accessible due to exhorbitant ticket prices, and the insurmountable hurdle of some of them being dead, lots of fans find themselves happily entertained by talented musicians who simply mimic their idols. They don't always look like the real deal, but they try to.

It must be a funny old life devoting your talent to someone else's artistry. As well as getting the performance right, you have to...

He *was just getting* absorbed in it when his phone buzzed. Sighing with annoyance, he stretched over to his big, still-wet jacket and wrestled it from a top pocket. "Roddy here!" he said with an edginess unappreciated by the caller.

"Ken here!" he mimicked. "The Playhouse."

"What about it?" asked Roddy, suddenly sitting up straight.

"Be there within the hour."

"Why?"

"The chance of a lifetime, no less. That's why. So get your fucking skates on, my boy. Literally if necessary."

"Why?"

"The three-star show has lost its third Elvis. A badly broken leg. I've managed to sell you as a replacement prospect, but they wanna test you right now. Well, within the hour."

Roddy thought he must be dreaming. Stuff like this just didn't happen to him. "Am I dreaming?" he asked.

"It's a dream job if that's what you mean."

"Bloody hell. Fiona's got the car. I can't be so fast."

"Think big. I told you before. Call a cab."

"Are you serious? Is this some kind of practical joke? Don't be cruel."

"I'm serious. But I can't hold your hand. Too far away tonight. Ask for Sam Fantoni at the back door. He's got the other two tribute guys, the band and singers all set up for a try-out with you. There's no way you can miss this one, my friend. Just be there."

Roddy's fingers shook with sudden, adrenalin-powered excitement as he dismissed Ken's call with a brief "okay" and pressed the numbers for a taxi. In the time it would take to arrive, he'd fix up dog-sitting with Willie, his aged neighbour. Then look out the embroidered white suit that Angus had obviously spent thousands on. Then be on his way. In more ways than one.

Perhaps...

* * *

"Are you the stand-in guy?" The long-haired Scots roadie opening the cab door seemed to know what was happening. He paid the driver and took Roddy by an arm of his white jumpsuit – into which he'd just struggled en route – leading him up steps to the theatre's back entrance. The would-be star said: "I'm just a try-out prospect, I'm told. But I've high hopes you guys will go for me. My new Elvis career hasn't exactly set the heather on fire so far. But this could be my big chance." The helper rang a doorbell and kept him talking till the door opened and a red-suited man appeared, stretching a hand out in greeting: "Hi, Roddy! I'm Sam. Let's get this show on the road. Pronto. Our friend here can be the audience if he likes."

They all went inside and Roddy was hustled up to the stage to be introduced to his fellow musicians. They smiled, shook hands and made friendly chat, but got straight down to business. "Name a couple of numbers you'd like to start with," said Cooper.

Roddy picked two favourites that most suited his Elvis voice, one fast and one slow. "Blue Suede Shoes, maybe, and There's Always Me …are these good for you?"

"Yup, give us a starting note and we'll get the key." A few tuning sounds followed, the mic was raised to his mouth, the girls tested one or two supporting vocals, and he was off. As he found his voice, each song quickly found momentum, rolling along, with the others chiming in and gaining confidence in him with each phrase. Soon, they were all having a heady ball. Someone in the dark of the front stalls was taking pictures – of a magic moment worth capturing. And when the rockers were done, it was raised thumbs and smiles all round. "Was that okay?" asked a red-faced Roddy of no-one in particular.

"More than okay!" said Sam, emerging from stage right. Bouncing across the very boards that had just seen the unfortunate bounce of braveheart Krish. "Tomorrow morning we'll rehearse your full

repertoire. Gotta trust you to get it right first time; ready for the show at night. But we'll take the chance. Come backstage right now and I'll write you a holding note. A mini-contract between you and me for the next couple of shows. But…"

Then came Sam's big question that broadened Roddy's already-big smile: "If you think we're good for each other, would you be free to join us on the coach for the six-week tour of England we still gotta do?" It raised all kinds of questions in his mind, mainly about money, his wife's reaction and his dog's welfare, but Roddy found himself saying, just like that: "Of course I'm free."

"Where the hell am I?" Krish woke up to find four of his showmates around his bed in the room now officially vacated by Sam – now back unofficially, in standing room only. Special leave had been given for him to bring in the two other Elvi and a singer. For five minutes only. It was a moment they had to grab – not just to show concern for their fallen star but also to chart a way ahead for the show. They didn't want to add to his pain – he was still groaning – but things had to be explained, planned and sorted.

"You're in hospital after a bad fall, Krish," said Sam. "Your leg's twice broken. Ain't no chance you can get back soon and see the tour through. It's fifteen English dates over six weeks. We're so sorry to tell you this…" He shot a glance at the others, who all agreed with a rumble adding up to a collective "Yeah".

Was that a teardrop on the big guy's unshaven cheeks? He managed to say, in barely a whisper, "Ok, I get it… reckon I'll just have to fly home to Boston."

Sean stepped forward and gripped one of his shoulders, to help him be strong. "You can't do that either, Krish. There's no flying for you for as many as twelve weeks. While you heal. You just gotta stick around here."

"Here? In hospital?"

"No." Sam thought he'd better take over as the bad-news reader. "You can only stay here for three more days."

"Then what? Then where do I go?"

"We're still working that one out," said Sam, who noticed his own crossed fingers.

"You got another guy to step in?" whispered Krish.

"Yeah, he's kinda new to the Elvis act but we reckon he'll hack it."

"What's his name?"

At that very moment the blonde nurse bustled into the room – smiling, though her very presence said the session had to end. She made shooing gestures, as if to waft them out. But Sam managed to say: "Kirkwood. Roddy Kirkwood."

The nurse threw a hand across her well-rounded lips and gasped. They all turned to look at her.

"You know him?" asked the girl singer.

"Know him?" She stared back in wide-eyed astonishment. "He's my husband."

As her legs buckled she fell on to the edge of Krish's bed, causing him to bellow with pain.

And what she learned in their next five-minute allowance drove her to seek out a hotel for the night.

Chapter 14

All is revealed

"Where the hell are you? Please answer your phone!" It was 2.30am, he'd chalked up fourteen missed calls to Fiona, but now, on the cusp of his day of days – intense rehearsals, his first big-time show, a confession that finally *had* to be made – his wife had chosen not to come home. She should have appeared an hour ago. Already exhausted after his mini audition and hours awake in bed, he felt desperately helpless. Until his phone finally lit up.

It was Sam, offering no apology for the hour and for not being Fiona; getting right to his point: "Look, Roddy, your domestic life really ain't none o' my business, but your fitness for today sure is. We didn't know your good lady didn't know. We met her at the hospital by chance. I gotta tell you she knows now and she ain't a happy bunny. In the interest of you getting some sleep, I'll say only two words: Dunberry Hotel." The phone went dead again before Roddy could say "Thanks".

So she knew! He felt alarmed and cheated. At not having

the chance to tell it his way. She would also feel alarmed and cheated, and wouldn't understand. Not immediately anyway. Would she ever come home again? At least he knew now she was alive and well. He'd have to try to sort things out somehow, sometime tomorrow (or rather, later today). But when? They were both set to be rather busy. He groaned the longest of groans as he shut his eyes to focus on his story and its looming challenges. But the eyes had other ideas. Within a minute, he had slumped back on the pillow and fallen into a deep sleep... with *Heartbreak Hotel* playing somewhere in the back of his brain.

On the No 26 into town, joining the honest travellers to honest work – and feeling almost like one – he parked his wrapped guitar near the *Metro* newspaper box and picked out a copy to relax and divert his brain. It did anything but, as he found a seat and pushed into it against a big, black-coated lady in the next berth. "Jesus Christ!" he exploded as he took in the headlines...

THE NEW KING OF SCOTLAND

Our man rocks up to save US Elvis show

She turned, appalled, but Roddy was even more shocked as he clocked the attached picture. It could only have been him, rocking on the stage yesterday in full Presley gear. "How the bloody hell did that happen?" he said, out loud again. To explain himself, he pointed at the image and said: "That's me." The woman stood up abruptly, said "Excuse me" in an aggrieved Morningside tone, and pushed out into the aisle to press the bus's stop button.

Roddy's sleepy eyes did not even see her stepping off. They were now staring in disbelief at the story below the headline:

The American Elvis has left the building... but our man has taken his place.

It happened during rehearsals for the "Kingsize Elvis" spectacular hitting the big city this weekend.

Krish Ray, one of the show's big three star US tribute acts, suffered a dramatic fall during rehearsal at the Edinburgh Playhouse, badly breaking a leg.

It put him out of action for the rest of the production's UK tour. And while he underwent surgery at the Royal Infirmary, the call went out: "Who can replace him?"

Johnny Lee Memphis, Scotland's top Elvis tribute actor, was not available, so his chosen − but untested − protege, 40-year-old Roddy Kirkwood, was enlisted to don the famous white jumpsuit.

How will he do? Fans will find out tonight, on the first of a two-date run at The Playhouse. But Edinburgh-born Roddy himself − dubbed Roddy the Body − is keeping his fingers crossed.

"I'm just a try-out prospect," Roddy (pictured in action) told our reporter. "But I have high hopes these guys will go for me. My new Elvis career hasn't exactly set the heather on fire so far. But this could be my big chance."

He whistled with amazement as he raked a hand through his hair. He was shaken, but couldn't decide whether to feel proud or used. Judging by the quotes, "our reporter" had to be the long-haired "roadie" who received him at the theatre yesterday ...no doubt really the promoters' PR person, employed to cynically pump out a ticket-selling story. So the moment Roddy saw Sam in the dressing room, he waved the front-page splash under his nose, demanding: "Do you know something about this?"

Sam took the paper, scanned it, and smiled broadly, showing his full set of Hollywood teeth. "I wish I did, fella. What a superb piece of publicity. Worth a million dollars!"

"So who wrote it? Who took the picture?"

"Who wrote it, I dunno. But I saw your buddy taking pictures from the front stalls. You know, the guy you came in with."

"My buddy? I thought he was your man."

Sam looked unusally thoughtful, removing his cap to scratch his balding head. "I think what we have here my friend, is the proverbial ambulance-chaser. I reckon it's an enterprising hack who wormed his way in after spotting the mercy men at work."

"I feel violated... or something," said Roddy.

"I suggest you just grin and bear it," Sam said, trying to keep a straight face. "A guaranteed full house can't be bad. Now please get out your little banjo and give us a wee tune, as your old Scotch daddy might have said... and done."

"Uh-huh," he grunted in Elvis style, getting into the spoken accent before adopting it for the songs. "Ah reckon you're right, sir."

Sam handed over a chunky batch of pages with titles and lyrics. Some he knew, others he was expected to learn. Pronto. A moment to feel pretty thankful for his photographic memory. "Just get out there and get straight into them," said Sam. "Ain't no time to lose."

On stage, Roddy placed the notes on a nearby barstool, unbuckled his guitar and swung it over his shoulder. The first tuning ping of its E string prompted an instant echo from the keyboard player who threw him a wave and a smile: one of several who'd turned up in casual gear to give him musical and moral backing. Catching the spirit, Roddy became the centre of attention in what he was wearing – checked lumberjack shirt and jeans. Alongside the keyboard, there were a drummer, a bass guitarist and two of the backing girls already trilling with the tuning.

The next three hours, right up to the lunch break, were his. His to screw up, or his to triumph. Co-stars Sean and Cooper appeared now and again, nursing Starbucks paper cups and offering encouraging expressions, but didn't participate.

In the event, after he'd charged through a score of numbers from *Teddy Bear* to *Don't*, it seemed, to judge by the professionals' applause, that he'd pulled it off; seemed he could probably battle his way through all the star showmanship required of him tonight.

With a little help from his friends...

Not that there was a moment to wallow in it. The last note of *My Way* had barely faded when a real roadie was standing before him, a cup of steaming soup in one hand and a mobile phone in the other. "It's been ringing in the dressing room a few times," said the boy. "Could be urgent. Thought I'd better give you a chance to respond ...sir."

Facetime opened with Fiona, in her uniform, thrusting the morning paper at him, headline first. She was angrier than he'd ever seen her, and that was saying something. "Seems the whole world knows about your new career but you didn't think of telling your wife," she spat.

"You weren't there to explain to..."

"So-called wife."

"Where were you, my love? Oh, don't bother to tell me. At some sleazy hotel, I heard. Seems the whole world knew but me. Finally managed to snare one of your admiring doctors, eh?"

She ignored the jibe and thrust the paper up again. "Don't tell me you seriously gave up your good... well, goodish... job for THIS?"

"I didn't give it up. It gave me up."

"When was that?"

"A few weeks ago."

"What?"

"I've been trying to find the right moment to break it to you. Out of kindness."

"Kindness? You've been fooling me for weeks, pretending to go to work, while not really. What the hell have you been doing?" She thrust the paper into the screen again. "THIS?!"

"No, this is quite new."

"Ok." The newspaper had vanished now and he could see her red-nailed fingers in outrage mode on her hips. "So somebody somewhere just pounced on you – yesterday – saying you'd make a great Elvis Presley. How did it happen, for God's sake."

"I'll explain when I see you."

"Don't count on seeing me. Ever. Again. You've given me a lot to think about, Roderick."

"Baby, don't say don't..." he started, resisting the urge sing it, like he'd just been doing.

But the screen went blank.

Chapter 15

Everybody, let's rock

If his lady was seriously doubting him now, Roddy could beat that ...he hated himself. Hated his failure to make anything work – to make proper money – and his own diffident character that seemed to accept that. Or at least not to fight it hard enough. Which, paradoxically, seemed to make sense of what she called this "senselessly juvenile" move. He could be as bold as he liked in this character. Loud, extrovert, suggestive. All things were possible. Because it wasn't him. It was Elvis.

Which meant he-as-Elvis was really going to rock the boat. If he'd lost her already, what was there to lose? Having spent the afternoon in a dressing room marked "Krish" listening to, and learning, more tracks – and aping the King's sexy moves – he was ready to let the rock roll away his pain; for the moment at least. Ready to check out what another, more glamorous life would have been like. Ready, indeed, to let other women appreciate him... well, him-as-Elvis.

Even Sofia, the blue-eyed East European make-up girl,

seemed to value his new persona, as she warmed up his skin, pencil-blacked his brows and brushed down the makeshift sideburns he'd carved out of Fiona's black hairpiece. "Maybe you just dye your hair?" she said. "Would look more natural."

"Really? D'you think my own hair is strong enough?" He noted that she seemed to be a fan of hair-colouring herself, with her flowing auburn hair projecting streaks of silvery blue.

She lifted the wig for a moment and seemed to massage his scalp. "Maybe not," she said, with a wicked chuckle through full lips that, in their purpleness, showed an art-school colour sense also apparent in her long, sky-blue fingernails. "Maybe it need some gingering up."

"That's not funny."

"I mean, a tonic. You need a tonic."

"You can say that again," he said, almost suggestively. But she didn't rise to it, keen to preserve her professionalism and a certain modesty suggested by the high Victorian collar of her blouse.

"I'm done," she said, waving him out of the chair. He stood up before the mirror, curling a top lip in the glory of his new face and white jumpsuit, while she stood back to admire her work. "Needs one more thing," she said. "Something Krish left behind." The well-sculpted 28-year-old vanished behind a screen and reappeared with an elaborate cape matching the rest of his high-collared outfit. He almost blushed as she swung it around his neck and fastened it with a distinct air of familiarity. "Now you go," she said, pushing him out the door. "You go wow them."

"I could get used to this," he muttered to himself as he slowly made his way along an ill-lit corridor to the side of the stage. Nervous but relishing the throbbing, ever-louder music, and huge waves of applause. In the room he'd heard Cooper, as the early blue-jeaned Elvis, belt his way through classic numbers like *Hound Dog, Blue Suede Shoes* and *Heartbreak Hotel*. Now, the off-duty Cooper was coming to greet him and lead him nearer to the big sound of Sean doing his mid-Elvis in full leathers. "You okay, man?" said Cooper, grabbing Roddy's arm. "Don't worry, it's a great audience. Very loving."

Roddy clocked the red streaks on his face. "I can see that," he said. "You're covered in lipstick."

"Yeah. An occupational hazard, man. But you gotta play ball."

Roddy could hardly hear his next question of over the last note of *Now or Never*. "In what way d'you mean?"

Cooper was bellowing now: "You gotta kiss 'em back. Indulge their fantasy. And they ain't always the ladies you'd choose to kiss either. The trick is to keep it kinda light, no pressing or heavy hugging. They gotta know the singing comes first. Unless of course..."

"Unless what?"

"Unless nothing. Don't pay me no mind, man. You'll find out for yourself." They could hear Sean bowing out in a thunder of applause and screams. "I think your moment has come."

Roddy heard Sam, wearing his compere hat, explain Krish's absence – then sing the praises of "The New King of Scotland" while waving that morning paper's headline in front of the huge gathering of a thousand fans. A slight groan of disappointment was followed by a big cheer for "your own Roddy Kirkwood... or Roddy the Body!". And he was on. Cooper pushed him, Sean pulled him, handing over the mic, and Sam's clapping welcome merged into that of the crowd and an introductory crescendo from the band. Somebody said "break a leg, man!" but its awful irony didn't register.

It was all dizzying. Spotlights played on to his face, almost blinding him, then he could suddenly see... In front of him, an ocean of faces with phones and eyes lit up like stars; behind him a great rocking band; to his left four glamorous backing singers, and above him a huge cinema screen showing his face in close-up like some kind of movie star. It all added up to one thing: he had to deliver. And how...

"Hello, Edinburgh, ma ain home toon," he said in an exaggerated Scots accent, to a big cheer; before changing to Deep South, a la the original: "Ah'm gonna be recallin' the final phase of Elvis, when he sang more ballad-type songs. But even in his Las Vegas concert days, he liked to recall his first days as a raw rocker. So if you don't mind, ladies and gennelmen, I'm gonna start with *Won't You Wear My Ring...*"

To get an objective view of his new man in action, Sam moved to the back of the auditorium, taking in the whole scene. What he saw and heard made the old cynic gasp. The voice was incredibly near to the original, the basso nearly-profundo phrases playing against the high tenor ones with stunning precision,

But there was more....

Roddy's moves were immaculately similar to the King's. The nervous leg shaking, the squatting, the judo kicks, the swirling around under the cape, the caressing of the mic.

But there was more...

The audience reaction was almost hysterical. With each song, from *Teddy Bear* through *There's Always Me* to *Can't Help Falling*, their appreciation grew in volume. The sea of heads, mainly grey, swayed from side to side in a high degree of ecstasy. Sam heard himself saying, "God almighty, Elvis lives."

As Roddy hit his final note of *My Way*, amid a tsunami

of applause, tears and cheers, a score of red-faced women besieged the stage and shot out imploring, searching hands. He responded with a recently practised move: whipping off and throwing out a series of faux silk scarves with a flourish.

It was almost a bullfighting technique, elegantly holding off the attacker with a stylised gesture, as advised by Johnny Lee, who was well used to such adoration; and who had noted that "if this happened the other way round with male fans groping a female singer, the guys would be arrested".

When the scarves were exhausted, Sam was back; among the fans, in full voice. "Who wants to kiss Roddy?"

"Oh, fuck," said Roddy, and the expletive was broadcast if thankfully drowned by the fuss.

"Form an orderly queue," added Sam.

Between lingering fragments of *My Way*, Roddy bowed down to every outstretched mouth and tried to plant one as lightly as possible. He reckoned he must have been through thirty of these swooning souls when, thankfully, the last one appeared. Was this a Muslim lady? She swept her face-and-head covering aside, and he coughed as he saw it was... Fiona! He stopped in mid-phrase, pulled back in astonishment with blacked-up brows that seemed to say: "What are you doing here?"

"I don't want a kiss," she said. "I just think we should talk."

"Ok," he managed, covering over the mic, "better come backstage when we're done."

Somehow, when they were done, she got there: Back through the theatre foyer festooned with Elvis-themed posters, T-shirts, CDs and waves of chattering, exiting fans. Down the lane by the side of the building. To the back Stage Door bearing not just that title emblazoned on a blackboard but the claim that

The world's greatest artists have passed and will pass through here. The door where, only the day before, her husband had been hustled into *his* limited degree of stardom. To which, she now conceded, he seemed better suited than she had imagined. She couldn't deny Roderick had put on an impressive show (for those who liked that kind of thing); but still felt quite out of place joining a crowd of fans hoping for star favours – autographs, selfies, one-to-one chats – with a few perhaps offering to extend some.

A roadie opened the stage door and called out: "Is there a Fiona Kirkwood here?" She raised a hand, got a thumb's up, and was ushered through a parting sea of envious eyes.

"Hya, honey," said Roddy, when she was brought to him in the room still marked "Krish"; he put down the guitar he'd been idly strumming and tried not to look amazed. "Great you could make it! Did you use that ticket I got for you?" He noticed Sam and the others watching but hanging back, as if expecting a small nuclear war. They surely reckoned, after all, that she would not be happy with a) her husband's new career, and b) their plan to whisk him away from home for many weeks.

"Of course," she said with a half-smile. "You don't think I'd pay for rubbish like this, do you?"

He looked hurt. "You didn't like my set then?"

"It was OK, I suppose. But not my kind of music, as you know."

"What are you doing here then?"

"Curiosity," she said. "Pure and simple. My nose was bothering me."

"I suppose that explains the hibab? Or the hi, babe, as I like to put it." He chuckled at his own witty wordplay; but she just kept half-smiling.

"I had to make it up myself," she said, unpeeling the dark red scarf from her chin and head. "I'd intended to come incognito but, guess what, someone had removed my black wig. And my black eyebrow pencil. I wonder who that might have been?" She laughed a little, then added: "Anyway, you can rest assured, my dear, I haven't converted to Islam overnight. Though you seem to have converted from ordinary guy to berserk fantasist."

"I didn't expect you to approve."

"No, but I have to admit it beats your usual boring self," she said grudgingly. "So I suppose I ought to congratulate you... though, as I say, it's not my cup of cultural tea."

"You might like this then," he said, digging a hand into a pocket of his white Bill Belew creation, and handing her a fat little beige envelope.

"What is it?" she asked, gripping her elegant fingers around it.

"A thousand smackers."

"Pardon?" As her jaw dropped, Roddy gestured over to Sam, who returned a wink aimed at both.

"From the boss, who says it's just a down payment. For services expected to be rendered."

"It's your fee then... for two nights?" asked Fiona.

"No, it's yours. Well ours, I suppose. But I won't be here to help you use it."

"Use it? For what?"

"One month's accommodation."

"For me? Where? For who?" Fiona's puzzlement grew as Roddy began explaining...

"For Krish, my predecessor." He grinned and pointed to the "Krish" sign on the door.

Her jaw dropped again. As did the envelope, right to the floor. At which point, Sam stepped in, picked it up, and intervened, saying: "Maybe I should explain, Mrs... can I call you Fiona? As we kinda know each other, after meeting at the hospital...you remember?"

"I suppose so." Fiona thought he was familiar but her memory wasn't working too well.

Sam picked up the envelope and explained: "As our Krish's gonna be immobile and unflyable for a couple of months anyway, Roddy and I kinda thought it would be a smooth transition for him, from hospital – where you've been caring for him anyway – to your home, for that duration."

"My home? Why my...our... home?"

"Well, Roddy tells me your daughter is off to the Americas and has left her room unoccupied. Also, you being a nurse, you can keep a professional eye on our man."

"Are you crazy?"

"It's a win-win situation," said Roddy, "as the promotion company doesn't want to keep him in an expensive hotel for all that time, and we could use the kind of money they *are* prepared to spend. But it's just an idea. It's up to you."

Sam clutched the beige envelope to his chest under a beatific, imploring Hollywood smile. "Think of it, Fiona. Roddy's out there making a grand a show, you're holding the fort back here making an extra grand a month."

He placed the envelope gently into her hands again, and she seemed to cautiously accept it. "This is for one month," he said. "There will be more, pro rata, for as long as the arragement lasts. Can we count on you?"

Roddy and his wife exchanged looks that seemed to say it might work. He nodded encouragingly and, after a pregnant pause, she simply said: "You bastards!"

Chapter 16

Out-of-action man

"Hey, mornin' guys!" Exuding forced bonhomie through his movie star dentals, Sam was already at Krish's bedside when the Kirkwoods arrived, with Fiona due to start work anyway and wondering at the US colonisation of her territory. He got straight to the point of their meeting: "Now that Krish is more or less compos mentis, I reckon we otta go over the future arrangements with y'all."

Wearing a flimsy and unflattering hospital gown, Krish smiled at the others wanly. The plastered-up leg was suspended and still giving him bad pain. He tried to stretch out a quivering arm to shake hands, but the couple sensed they should stretch to him, while Sam noted how less-than-glamorous his (out of) action man was today...unshaven and unusually tousled even unto his genuinely black Elvis sideburns. For these, and his normally shiny hair and tanned looks, he clearly had to thank some Indian blood somewhere.

His bungee-jumping confidence seemed to have survived

the accident, with his natural cockiness still showing as Roddy's handshake followed Fiona's (met with a smouldering look). "Real nice to meet you, Roddy," he managed with a weakened voice. "Sam says you gave a great performance last night... after stealin' ma job an' all. For that, I just gotta steal your life ...and your wife, no?"

Fiona threw a hand across her face and gasped in shock ...that anyone could think, let alone say, such a thing. Roddy's mouth fell open too, before he forced out a little chuckle and returned a playful: "Just try that, buddy, and you'll have *two* broken legs." He added a thin smile that said "We're joking, aren't we?" but both were already thinking their potentially sensitive relationship could have got off to a better start.

Sam coughed to attract attention and fill the ensuing awkward silence. "Just to be clear, folks, this deal is purely business, nothing personal involved."

"I should think so too," said Fiona in her best Edinburgh lilt. "Can I ask if Krish... er, Mr Ray... is now fully acquainted with the arrangements?"

The patient extended a weak arm again as if to pacify everyone, then said: "I am, ma'am. As I understand it, when I am discharged from here in a couple of days, you will transport me to your homestead. Where I'm gonna have your daughter's vacated room for a couple of months. Plus some help with getting food in. Plus I get your nursing services if and when required." His wife didn't seem to see it, but Roddy could have sworn Krish winked at that point.

"Did you just wink there?" he challenged him.

"You both gotta forgive my Boston sense of humour," said the patient.

"I didn't know Bostonians had a sense of humour," countered Roddy.

"Oh, they do, they do," said Krish. "Ever heard of the Boston Tea Party?"

"That wasn't funny."

"No, maybe not for you guys, I reckon."

Roddy wasn't sure if he was getting along okay, or not, with Krish. There some friendly spirit in their banter, but a distinct edginess too. In any case, it was Fiona who was going to have to live with Roger the Lodger. And she made her position pretty clear as she took her leave with a brief: "Is that all, gentlemen? I ought to get to work."

There was another awkward silence after she closed the door with something close to a bang.

Sam broke the silence again, offering a chance for Krish to be straight-up nice; but he first addressed Roddy: "We were wondering about your jumpsuit. The white one's all you got, eh? Krish would like to offer you his black one" – his eyes addressed the patient – "wouldn't you, Krish?"

"Err, yeah..." he started.

"Because, as you know, Elvis often wore two outfits in one show."

"That's a nice offer," said Roddy. "I hadn't thought of that. I was thinking of getting more, like, advice on techniques and pitfalls and stuff from Krish."

"He'll get to that later," said Sam. "But in the meantime..."

"Yeah," said Krish. "We can't do a fitting here; the suit's in a hospital locker somewhere, but we'll get someone to dig it out before you go. And I reckon it'll fit fine. We're both built kinda the same, me and Roddy the Body. God, who thought that one up?"

"Not guilty as charged," said Sam stepping forward with an obvious smile of regret. "Sadly. I wish I had seen that one."

"Anyway, there's a small snag with the black suit," said Krish.

"What's that?" the others asked in unison.

"It's torn in two right up one leg and there's blood all over it. All part of the medics' service."

"Oh," they said in unison.

Sam looked at Roddy. "No black suit for tonight's big show then, baby. Looks like you're gonna be – again – all white on the night." He chuckled at his own clever wordplay.

"Yeah," said Roddy with a forced smile.

"Yeah," repeated the patient. "You're gonna need an invisible mender and an invisible cleaner. Apart from that, the suit's yours for the duration. I'd like it back, though. For when *I'm* back."

Sam put a final point on the thought with another of his inimitable wordplays. "Speakin' as one who's known real hardship," he said, "I reckon it's always good to be back in the black."

He laughed out loud, but neither of the others could even stretch to a groan.

It was an unfamiliar nurse who hustled them out of the room. Not before Krish had asked her, with a broad come-on smile, to look out his damaged suit and give it to Roddy. And not before he had rustled up some sincerity to reassure his replacement that "I'll be with you in spirit... call me any time for tips about the music ...and the women!" As they smiled and shook hands, Roddy wondered if their arrangement would prove to be a good idea. Did he really mean that Krish should "get well soon"? Perhaps "out of action" was the best place for this action man to be. He seemed a mite too interested in women.

* * *

In the cab back to town, Sam did his best to make Roddy feel better about his wife being at home alone ...except for the company of a sexual predator. "Aw, naw," he assured his new man, "he ain't nothin' like that. He has a real nice little lady back in Boston, and they're over the moon about each other." When he saw Roddy begin to relax, Sam's sense of mischief kicked in. "There's just one little problem..."

"Yeah, what's that?"

"All women think he's irresistible. Can't keep their hands off him. He finds it a bit of a problem; knows it comes with the territory professionally, but seems stuck with it personally as well. Makes 'em go on heat on sight. A big hunk o' love, as our Great Leader might say."

"Bloody hell," said Roddy. "Stop the cab. I think I want out."

Sam laughed — again — at himself and placated Roddy by grabbing his shoulder. "C'mon, man," he pleaded. "I'm just kidding. He ain't like that at all. And there's no way you can get out anyway. We need your love tonight! You just gotta understand my New York humour."

"Oh, like I have to understand the Boston humour. Can't say I find either of them very funny."

Which Sam seemed to find even funnier.

Paid with a handful of notes, the cab driver dropped the still-chuckling American at The Playhouse and drove on to Portobello. He waited while Roddy left a letter for Fiona, said a fond farewell to Shep being handed over to neighbour Willie, and packed up a bag of fresh clothes and toiletries. Which then joined a suitcase carrying, aptly, the famous suits. Then it was back to town, big-time performance and his new life. After the show, he'd spend a hotel the night with the others to get used to the rhythm of the game, then set off with them by double-deck bus in the morning. To more than twenty venues all over England….from Newcastle to Nottingham to Manchester and beyond. There was something about Manchester that rang a bell. Something about Nottingham too...

Chapter 17

On the road

"Who's got a big bust?" Fiona's first phone call to him aboard the old Alexander Dennis double-decker was full of suspicion. Exhausted after a second acclaimed performance, Roddy's overworked voice was now weakened and slurred, against a background of more grinding rock music, so he reckoned it was forgivable that she'd have misheard it.

But it was indeed a big bus. Ploughing its dinosauric way down the slushy A1 motorway towards Newcastle; equipped with all manner of customised comforts: sofas, beds, drink cabinets, sound system, TV, microwave, wifi, male and female lavatories, and arty rugs. All designed to let the talented team catch their breath between energy-sapping gigs. And they were all lounging about in T-shirts, making the most of it.

There was the occasional big bust too, but a wiped-out Roddy hardly noticed.

"No, honey, I'm saying it's a big bus... a huge double-decker."

"Oh. Like a London bus?"

"Dunno, same colour anyway. Red, with all not-so-mod cons, lots of home comforts, including some incredible pychedelic rugs."

"Drugs!" she exclaimed. "I knew it. You're all spaced out there in a...mobile den of iniquity full of Americans."

"No, no, dear. You keep mishearing me. Rugs. I said rugs, as in carpets."

"Oh."

"I'm actually just reading a book right now. Well, looking at the pictures."

"What kind of dodgy pictures?"

"Oh, please. It's just a biography about ...guess who?"

"Elvis. You're completely obsessed."

"Well, his legacy could help us make a good living, no?"

"So I suppose I'd better ask how it went last night? I got your goodbye letter, thanks. But you really didn't have to dash away like that."

"Just wanted to claim a perk of the job. One hotel night before it might all go wrong. Though, yeah, my set seemed to go okay, I think. The others said so anyway. And the fans. They get a bit over-enthusiastic ...and over-amorous."

"I noticed that. It's as well you can keep yourself under control. You can, can't you?"

"Ouch!" he exclaimed as the coach went over a bump. But that wasn't the sole cause of his little fright. A comb was being tugged through his hair, which was now in the process of being dyed – to jet black from sandy. "Sorry," said a female voice, which put Fiona on red alert.

"Who was that and what's happening?" she demanded.

"It's just Sofia," said Roddy. "The team's make-up lady who thinks my natural hair could work on stage just so long as it's black."

"So I take it you'll be sending my wig back? And maybe even my ring, eh? I've heard Sofia is beautiful."

Roddy cleverly redirected the thought. "We both heard that, on that Amsterdam trip many moons ago ...remember? When a drunk guy in the pub kept saying 'Sofia is beautiful!' Turned out he was a Bulgarian talking about his capital city."

"So how beautiful is this Sofia? And is she Bulgarian too?"

"Well, she is Bulgarian, as it happens..."

"That wasn't my first question. I said how..."

His head was suddenly plunged into a basin of dye and he couldn't answer from the depths of it. When he resurfaced, Fiona was asking the question again, adding: "Fancyable, is she?" But he changed the subject...

"Talking of which, how's your glamorous but knackered lodger?" gulped Roderick.

"No idea. He's not with with us for a couple of days yet."

"And the dog...how's Shep?"

"I think he's missing you already."

"Aw. And you?"

"Maybe. Next time it's Facetime. Just to see your new hair and check out what you're up to."

"See you then," they echoed to each other.

Twenty minutes of scalp-rubbing later, Sofia shaded her blue eyes, backed off with a sweet smile, a conclusive "there!" and collapsed into her easy chair. "What you think? You think maybe your wife will like you no longer ginger?"

Sean, their middle Elvis, called out from his sofa: "Yeah, man, she'll love the new you!" And early-Elvis Cooper raised a glass of something offering "hear, hear, ma boy!" with a big grin. There was already a ton of camaraderie in the group, and that wasn't even counting the friendly English backing singers who had shed their sparkly dresses but still looked pretty good relaxing in casual gear, he noted,

He stared into a hand-held mirror and barely recognised himself. Which feeling he was starting to get used to. This was, after all, Elvis, and the black – otherwise natural – hair and unapologetic sideburns definitely seemed to work. At the very least this would be vastly preferable, of course, to that ill-fitting Cher wig.

"We will try it tonight," said Sofia, noting Roddy's widening eyes and quickly adding so as not to be misunderstood: "And put away the good lady's wig."

"Yeah, we'll try it tonight!" Sam swivelled his head back from the drink cabinet, offered Sofia a little hand-clap, turned down the background music, and swayed his way to the driver's cab. Less than a minute later, the big dinosaur of a coach began to slow, as over its intercom system, he announced: "Boys and girls, we're about to leave the fair land of Scotland and enter the unfair land of England. Just joking of course, girls! But some of us here might want to record the change of country, so we'll stop for a while and anyone who wants to take a photo of the Welcome sign – with or without you in it – should grab the chance now."

At which point, the bus came to an abrupt layby halt and several bodies flew forward. Four of whom struggled out to record their presence under the big roadside sign that said *Welcome to England*, with the sub-line *Northumberland*.

The driver, a Scottish one-time cabbie called Hamish, turned off the ignition and waited. Stretching his legs without actually facing the elements, Roddy came over to talk to him, and after a few exchanges about the weather being "not great for driving" noted a little pile of paper strips above the glove compartment. The lettering on them said "Roddy the Body" so – he reckoned – they could be something to do with him. "What are these for?" he asked Hamish.

"For legal safeguarding," said not Hamish, but Sam.

"Well, all the three-Elvis posters on display all over the towns we're visiting have two of the stars' names correct, but – as you know – the third one is no longer with us. And you are..!"

"So we have to flag up the change so that the fans don't turn up and get disappointed at Krish's absence and maybe demand their money back or even get into legal stuff."

"Are you saying they'd be disappointed with me?" Roddy asked wanly.

"Naw, naw," said Sam. "It's just to be on the safe side. Nobody would ever be disappointed with a talent like yours. But we gotta beat off the clever guys who think they can catch us out. So..."

"So," said Hamish, waving a batch of the paper strips, "when we get into Newcastle today, I've got the real fun task of changing Krish's name to yours on all the posters I can find with these wee stickers. Same for every town we hit."

"Get it?" said Sam.

"I get it," said Roddy.

But the boss wasn't finished. "There's just one more thing, Roddy. We managed to sell you pretty well in Scotland as a life-saving local hero, but I don't reckon that'll work here. Among these ...what d'you call 'em?"

"Sassenachs."

"Yeah, that's right, Braveheart. But the point is, here they're expecting a triple bill of real full-time Americans. So you gotta talk our tongue at all times. Like you're straight outta Tupelo, cradle of the King. Can you do that?"

Roddy turned it on hard: "Ah sure can, buddy. That ain't no kinda problem for this boy. But I can do better than that."

"How?"

"My folks come from Moray, a county at the top of Scotland, and there's a village there called Dallas. I've been there a coupla times."

Sam showed his gleaming white teeth again and patted his new man's new black hair. "That'll do for me," he said, as he acknowledged the others clambering back in. "You're straight outta Dallas. So let's get this show on the road again."

Hamish turned the ignition key but the sound that came back was a weak cough. He looked at the others and expelled a groan of frustration. Somehow, the big battery had drained and the cold weather wasn't going to help it recharge itself. Anxious eyes focused on Hamish as he tried again and again to get the engine going. There wasn't much time to spare and the emergency services would take a fair while to reach them.

"Only one thing for it," said Sam, rolling up his metaphorical sleeves and summoning all the assembled company to do the same. "We've gotta give this thing a push start. Everybody out! We're gonna heave the beast over the Border." There was a long, loud general sigh, but...

All twenty of them – seven singers, five band members, and eight support staffers – congregated around the rear of the coach then put their collective shoulders to it. As it began to move, a perspiring Cooper turned to Roddy and said in an exaggerated American twang: "What the hell are we doin' takin' the bus...? The bus is supposed to take us."

Just as they crossed the Border, with angry traffic sounding off behind them, Hamish let out the clutch, the engine burst into life, and the whole gang burst into relieved laughter. It was

Roddy's first trip on the Elvis Tour coach and a moment he knew he'd never forget.

Suddenly, feeling nostalgic about the leaving of his native land, Hamish burst into Scotland's most globally famous song – and threatened to murder it without mercy. Roddy felt compelled to step forward and help him out. As did the two other Elvi. Not to mention two of the females backing singers. Then it sounded pretty good, thought Roddy, though these bloody foreigners had very little right to sing it.

> *Should auld acquaintance*
> *Be forgot*
> *And never brought to mind*
> *Should auld acquaintance*
> *Be forgot*
> *For the sake of*
> *Auld Lang Syne*

As they finished it off with a long harmonised note, cheers, clapping and much laughter, he had to concede that they had to be forgiven for being so damned tuneful.

He also had to admit it was another memorable moment. That, and...

Pushing a double-decker bus from Scotland to England indeed!

What did they look like? Two tartan-scarfed fellas and a Bulgarian beauty sneaking around the streets of Newcastle in the light of the moon: Roddy, Hamish and Sofia dashing, in their softest of trainers from poster to poster, pasting Roddy the Body strips over the name of Krish Ray. Twice they stood quickly at attention as a slow-moving police car drove past, oozing suspicion. But it wasn't only the paste that was bonding. "I like Roddy the Body strips," said Sofia at one point, and both men looked at her with wide, enquiring eyes. She just smiled back sweetly, enigmatically.

Chapter 18

Lonesome tonight?

Newcastle hadn't rocked like that since the Luftwaffe rained bombs on it. Now, on the Sunday after the night before, it was strangely quiet. Nothing moved on the early-morning streets. Except the dino double-decker. As a wise precaution, just in case, Hamish had parked it on a hill near their hotel. But thanks to his prayers, it ignited instantly at the turn of its key.

With the band's City Hall night done and dusted and a long drive to Derby Arena ahead, there was a day off to be spent on the bus. Even into the free evening. And it occurred to Roddy, sitting at the lower-deck piano stool, that this was also Fiona's night off. They'd never actually gone out much, but had always liked being quietly at home when she wasn't dealing with blood, drama and distress. In fact, he noticed that even his fellow rockers were enjoying some peace. The bus engine was the loudest thing to be heard. Cooper of Portland, Oregon, and Sean of New York City played cards, while the girls were upstairs reading or messing about with each other's make-up.

It seemed like a good time to make the call, so he did. But not before covering his head with one of the red scarves that were flourished out to adoring fans. And there she was on the screen. His lady in matching red – and blue jeans – no longer the strict, uniformed nurse. Smiling and hugging Shep and saying: "Hi! Say hello to your dog."

"Hello, my dog," he said ...and, recognising his voice if not his face, Shep barked and whined and stuck his tongue out through what seemed a big grin.

"You been a good fella?"

He seemed to nod his head positively and Roddy added: "And your Mum – has she been good too?"

The dog didn't seem to reply, which oddly alarmed him, before she stepped in with: "Of course. And you?"

"Of course," he repeated.

"So why are you calling, other than to annoy me?"

"Well, you wanted to see my new black hair."

"Ok, show me then..."

The couple's conversation had been overheard. From the back of the bus, as if rehearsed, the drummer boy from Illinois – as he was known affectionately in the band, though he was actually Tim Bell from Bromley – gave a long roll on his single practice snare drum. Surprised but undaunted, Roddy whipped off the towel with a dramatic "Taraaah!"

Fiona gasped: "I'm shocked. So I suppose that's what they call a shock of black hair, but..."

"But what?"

"Maybe I could get used to it. You look like Elvis Presley."

"That," said Roddy with undisguised sarcasm, "is actually the whole idea."

"But that means you don't look like you anymore."

"That should be a relief to you then, my love." Oh, he so

enjoyed their teasing banter.

"That's true," she said with a half-smile playing across her face. She loved their teasing banter too. Shep snuggled into her and turned the half-smile into a full one. "But I suppose Sofia's done a good job of changing you."

He looked around to see with relief that the make-up girl was not on the lower deck, but ignored the remark anyway. "So what are you planning to get up to tonight?" he asked.

"Well, certainly not sex and drugs and rock 'n' roll which seems to be your nightly agenda these days. I'm just taking our dog for a nice long walk by the beach. Then..."

"Just a minute," said Roddy. "I've got something to ask you." He put the phone down on the piano, got up and walked diagonally across the width of the bus to find an acoustic guitar leaning against the boys' card table. They couldn't fail to notice, set down their cards, and with twinkling eyes, followed him back to the phone. Which he up-ended against a book before finding a chord to start singing...

Are You Lonesome Tonight?
Do you miss me tonight?
Are you sorry we drifted apart?

The keyboard player sat down, pushed him along the stool and began tinkling the ivories while the others stepped forward to join in...

Does your memory stray to a bright sunny day
When I kissed you and called you sweetheart?

Not just the two other Elvises. Two of the four female backing singers had now been magnetised downstairs to add their little flourishes too...

Do the chairs in your parlour seem empty and bare?
Do you gaze at your doorstep and picture me there?
Is your heart filled with pain, shall I come back again?

And although she wasn't sure how to take all this, Fiona simply couldn't deny that it all sounded pretty lush. Magical harmonies seemingly directed by the King in his musical heaven. So much so that she added her own voice in with the others' on the closing phrase.

Tell me, dear, are you lonesome tonight?

As they all applauded each other, compliments flew. "Blimey," said the Bromley boy on drums, addressing Roddy. "Your old lady is just about as good as you, mate."

"Aye," said driver Hamish, who had heard everything without once turning his head from the road. "I'd bloody well hire her for the show too!"

Manager Sam emerged from what he called the John just in time to hear that. "Hey cool it, young man," he called out. "I'm the guy who does the hiring around here. And however good she is, I ain't takin' on two members of the same family."

"Oh no?" said Fiona from the phone screen. "Have you forgotten, Mr Fantoni, that you have already hired me?! As of this evening, I'll have the extra job gave me. Taking in and taking care of your injured colleague, Krish. Who'll be arriving soon by ambulance. So I won't be lonesome tonight, will I?"

"Oh yeah," said Sam and Roddy simultaneously. "Of course."

"Any messages for him that I can pass on?"

"Tell him Roddy's doing okay in his role," said Sam, "but lie to him if you like – saying nobody will ever be as good as him... says Sam." He winked at Roddy, who had his own message...

"And you can tell him from me that I'll be wearing his black jumpsuit tomorrow night. One of the girls who used to be a seamstress managed to repair it like nothing ever happened to it."

"Did you enjoy that then, Roderick?" His wife tried to

tease without sounding suspicious, but failed. "Was it Sofia again? The pride of Vulgaria...er, Bulgaria, stitching up your inside leg?"

Roddy groaned and Sam spoke out.

"Now, now, Mrs Kirkwood, don't be like that. Sofia is a good girl. And as far as I know, your Roddy is a good kinda guy too."

"They're well matched then, aren't they?"

Roddy groaned again, opened his mouth to protest, but she had gone. Invisible again. Just like those bloody rips in Krish's black jumpsuit.

Chapter 19

Hello, who are you?

Tired but triumphant, Roddy had kicked off his white cowboy boots, slumped into an easy chair and drawn a towel across his forehead. He'd earned applause to the elegant roof of Nottingham's Royal Concert Hall and, unusually, was awarding himself a five-star performance. The towel felt like a hood, softening the sharp lights around the make-up mirror, and Robin Hood, legendary citizen of these parts, came to mind as he closed his eyes, began to relish the peace and drift away...

When there was a little light knock on his dressing room door.

He groaned. Not another excited fan, he hoped, looking for a selfie, an autograph or maybe even a kiss. He'd already had enough of these, though he realised that they paid his wages. He pulled himself up and made for the door without opening it. "Who is it please?" he called out.

"Diana Kirkwood," came the reply, in a soft female whisper.

"Who's that then?"

"I think it's your sister."

"I don't have a sister."

"Well, actually, I think you do."

Had he already fallen into a dreamy sleep? He shook his head violently, noting oddly that it was a relief not to worry these days about Fiona's black wig flying off, and opened the door slowly with a fast-growing sense of trepidation.

He had almost forgotten what his original hair looked like; but here, suddenly, it had reappeared. She was a handsome woman, seemingly taller than him, but presumably because of her well-heeled, fur-trimmed boots – and his bootless feet. The slight wrinkles above her high cheeks only enhanced the clear green intelligence of her eyes. "Aren't you going to ask me in?" she said with a smile.

"I've seen you somewhere before, haven't I?"

"Maybe," she said.

Dumbfounded, he pointed silently at the seat he had just vacated and she sat with practised elegance, setting a bag on the floor beside it. "I came to thank you for the £1000 you sent me."

"So...it was you," he managed.

"Or I should, of course, thank your father."

"Yes, I..."

"Or our father... our father who art in Heaven, as they say." She chuckled a little and loosened the white silk scarf that covered the collar of a her grey suit and frilled blouse framing a pearl necklace. "Here, these are for you." As if from nowhere she produced a small posy of fresias.

"Oh, thank you," he said. "What did you say your name was?"

"Diana," she said, producing a glossy business card and

handing it to him. "Kirkwood." Indeed, it confirmed her identity:

> *Diana A. Kirkwood*
> *Managing Director*
> *Notts and Crosses*
> *Commercial Property*
> *kirkwood@nottcross.com*

Roddy gulped. He drew the towel across his forehead again, and spoke from under it. "Are you serious? Did I hear you saying my father, Angus, is – was – also your father?"

"You did."

Roddy pulled up a high-backed wooden chair and fell into it to calm his shaking knees. "Have you any proof?" He was suddenly accutely aware that the next few seconds were going to mark a major change in his life, certainly in the whole character of his family. He had always suspected Angus of being a bit of a dark horse but this was beyond anything he had imagined... Could it possibly be? A sibling about whom he had known nothing for much of a lifetime? And if true, someone he'd have been over the moon to have known through his growing-up years. And yet it wasn't too late to make up for lost time. If true...

Diana leant over the side of her chair and opened her handbag. From it, she pulled a rolled-up official-looking paper. Unrolling it over her lap, she beckoned Roddy to have a look. It was, he saw, a birth certificate from the year 1980, and she pointed to the names it recorded. There was her name again, with the middle name Agnes. Under *Mother*, it said: Joanna Blythe, secretary; and noted as *Father* was Angus Donald Kirkwood, musician.

"How old does that make you now then?"

"I think I'm about two years older than you. So if our father met your mother after the liaison with my mother, there's nothing to be embarrassed about."

"I'm not embarrassed," said Roddy. "Just amazed. Why would he have kept you secret... from my mother and me... and you to some degree?"

"I think he was probably just too shocked to handle it all. I reckon he lived with Joanna and the baby me for only a few months before it all went wrong."

Roddy sighed, put the paper down under the mirror's lights and examined it closely. "Are you absolutely sure this is the right Angus Kirkwood? I know it's not a common name, but..."

"I'd be happy to have a DNA test done if you like," said Diana. "But I think this" – she pulled another piece of paper from her bag – "might convince you."

Roddy took it from her and saw only a blur. "What am I looking at?" he asked.

It was a yellowing newspaper cutting from 1979. "I'll read it for you if you like," she said. "But it's important to remember that your father – our father – was a bagpipe instructor in Canada, in British Columbia, at the time."

"Okay. Go..."

She read the headline first: "Canadian bands pipe up a storm at world pipe championships." Then went on...

For Canadians, there can now be no more important day in pipe band history than August 12, 1979, in Nottingham, England. On that day two non-UK bands, both from British Columbia, finished in the top six – Triumph Street and City of Victoria, fifth and sixth respectively. The latter's pipe tutor, Angus Kirkwood, said that, despite now planning to stay put in the UK, he was "absolutely delighted and extremely proud of these great musicians".

"Wow," said Roddy. "That's pretty convincing. I do remember Dad saying that he came back home to Britain in 1979. The naughty old bugger. Met and made your mum pregnant in Nottingham – and mine in Edinburgh – within about eighteen months of each other. So where's your mother now?"

"Sad to say she died about four years ago, just before I started trying to catch up with you."

"How did you do that, by the way? I recall seeing someone closely resembling you at Angus's funeral. Was that you? And how did you know about it?"

"As you say, I reckoned that he probably picked up his life back in Scotland and that latterly, considering his age, he'd be popping off soon. So I kept checking *The Scotsman* obituaries online. Until his name and story finally appeared. Which meant of course that, although I'd probably traced him, I could no longer visit him. Sadly, I could only show up at his funeral."

"Where we almost met."

"By which time, of course, I knew your name and kept it in mind until – still checking online news – I saw you'd hit the Elvis industry big-time. Soon to visit Nottingham on tour. So here I am!"

"But," said Roddy. "Why didn't you just come and talk to me at the funeral?"

"I really don't know," she said, nervously fingering her necklace. "I kept asking myself that after the event. It just seemed the wrong moment to hit you with a long lost sister in the middle of such an emotional event. Plus, I was just frozen with fear about the possibility we wouldn't take to each other. Just lost my nerve, I suppose."

Roddy stood up and held his arms out inviting her to be wrapped in them. "Well, I hope, dear sister, that I can now unfreeze your fear ...that we can get along just fine. Let me warmly welcome you into my family."

Diana stood up, dabbed some tears with her scarf and allowed herself to be enveloped. From the depths of their hug, she said: "You ought to know it's not just me expanding your family. I've got a husband and two beautiful daughters who'll be delighted to learn they've got a new uncle."

"And aunt!" said Roddy. "I must get on Facetime and tell my wife about this."

Fiona seemed to sense what had transpired the moment a bright-smiling Diana was guided into the Facetime frame. "I want to introduce you to somebody special," said Roddy; but his wife was already ahead of him.

"Don't tell me," she said, teasing her hair and brushing down her uniform to look her best. "This charming lady is a long lost sister?"

"How did you know?" they asked in unison.

"You look like twins," she laughed, then, addressing Roddy, said: "Please do introduce us."

"This is Diana, the product of my father's first relationship back in the UK... in Nottingham, where we are tonight. She tracked me down backstage and gave me the fright of my life."

"Yes, I can imagine," said Fiona. "Fright or not, what a wonderful moment for you both."

"It was certainly that, I can say," said Diana. "And I'm so pleased to meet you too."

Busy as she was, still at work, Fiona found the time to be delighted, friendly and welcoming, before noting: "I'm sure we didn't know – did we, Roderick? – that Angus was a dad before he met your mum?"

"Aye, quite a surprise."

"Your old man has been full of surprises for us since he died," she then said to Diana ...who laughed nervously and added: "Yes, I can see that."

"He had unusual interests, we've discovered. Not to mention a roving eye obviously."

"Well, I suppose it's yes again," said Diana.

"I rather trust that character trait doesn't run in the family blood, eh Roderick? Especially in the face of so many temptations these days."

At which point, the dressing room door flew open and make-up girl Sofia appeared, saying she still had to clean up Roddy's face. Seeing she was interrupting something, she quickly withdrew, mouthing "Sorry" and closing the door behind her. But the damage was done.

"She was just doing her job," said Roddy to the screen; but already it was blank.

He turned to Diana with a wry smile and said: "Suspicious mind!"

"Sounds like a cue for a song," she said with a chuckle, adding: "I should go now, but I've something to give you first."

She dug into her bag again and brought out a little square brown-paper package which looked old, dog-eared and dusty. A corner of it had been opened to reveal it was a Super 8 film cassette. "I don't know what to do with this," she said, "but it could be interesting. I found it among my mother's things after she died." She pointed an elegant finger at the lower left corner of the package – where the fading ink of a fountain pen had once scribbled *Angus in 1979*. I suppose it could be converted by somebody to give us a little picture into our Dad's past."

"I suppose it could," said Roddy, accepting the packet, reopening the door, and seeing her out with a kiss. "I'll see what I can do with it. In the meantime, do take care and keep in touch. We'll have you up in Scotland ASAP. You are a fabulous discovery!"

"You too," she said, vanishing with a bright smile into a dark corridor.

Chapter 20

Life with the lodger

"What the hell is this, baby? Calls itself a burger but, hell, it's smaller than a cupcake. How can you guys stay alive on dwarf food like this?" Fiona thought she'd done well, detouring to find him a US-style treat from McDonalds. But, digging into the brown-paper bag to grasp the goods, Krish was unimpressed. Just as he'd been with all her catering so far. Unimpressed by the Scottish fish and chips, the Italian "New York" pizzas, the Indian chicken korma, and even the combined cultural genius of Bonnie Burritos. Okay, she thought, most of it had been bought rather than home-cooked, but it was all Edinburgh's finest.

"Sorry, Krish, I didn't agree to feed you like a king," she said, brushing down her uniform ready for another day's proper work. "Or even *the* king, as you people like to call him."

"Elvis liked burgers okay, but they were – I guess – rightly king-size." He chuckled at his own wit. "And what's this?" He lifted up the paper cup that came with it, opened its plastic lid, and sniffed its familiar odour.

"It's Coke," she said. "The clue is in the writing on the outside. You asked me to get you some."

"Oh, shit." He laughed a sarcastic laugh that made her feel small. "I didn't mean this kinda coke, honey. I meant the kind that keeps us creative types going. Didn't you get it?"

"Oh. How could I get that?"

"You're into drugs at work, no? Surely you..."

"Don't be silly." She sounded prissy even to herself; but wasn't going to feel ashamed of it. "I wouldn't ever approve of that anyway."

"Anyway," he repeated prissily, "I'm still in pain and the approved medicine has worn off."

"Too bad," she said, realising this was not her empathetic Nightingale self talking.

Krish had lost his Elvis looks and grown a beard within this first week of his ambulance arrival at Vandeleur Avenue. She shouldn't blame him, she thought, as he was incapacitated by a bloody great plaster round his leg. But his lounging back eating unliked food, watching 24-hour CNN, having no exercise, no reading and no urge to do anything other than sing Elvis songs was starting to touch her nerves.

He couldn't even entertain Shep with feeding or walking, so the sad old canine was still in the temporary charge of Willie the neighbour, whose vintage didn't allow for much walking either.

"You maybe got some rum to cheer this up a little?" Krish asked, poking a finger into the Coke.

"To cheer *you* up, you mean."

"Well, yeah, reckon that's what ah mean." He smiled cheekily, and she melted for a moment.

"We might have a little whisky somewhere, I suppose."

"Now you're talkin', baby!"

"Please don't call me baby," she said as she vanished for a moment and returned with an almost-full bottle of Johnnie Walker. "Just red label. We can't stretch to the black. Please note, I don't approve this either. Roderick assures me you boys in the band never touch alcohol. You only drink bottled water, he says." She opened the bottle grudgingly and splashed a little into his cup. He smiled again, with his eyes begging for more. He could see he wasn't going to get it, not without adding more charm anyway.

"He's right, of course. When we're on duty. But... talking of Roddy, have you spoken with your own mini-king lately?" He took a large swallow of the drink and grimaced at its lack of kick. "How *is* Roddy doing in my life?"

"As well as you're doing in his, I would imagine," said Fiona, thinking it looked more like Krish was in daughter Lorna's life, encircled as he was by girlish Nerflixian posters of young stars they'd never heard of.

"Not quite, honey," he responded. "I reckon I'm not enjoying all his privileges. While he's no doubt enjoying a few of mine."

Fiona saw her moment to lunge. "Would that perhaps include Sofia?"

"How d'you know about her? I ain't had nothin' with her."

"Are you sure about that? I keep hearing she's a really sweet, innocent young lady. Methinks some people protest too much. Just happens that she's boringly beautiful."

Krish sat up a little, coughed into another bite, and said: "You got some kinda problem with her and Roddy?"

"Maybe," said Fiona. "But if I do, I'm keeping it to myself. Just tell me how innocent – or not – she is. So that I get a real picture of things."

"Dunno, to be honest. Just like me, she's got a partner back home in ...wherever."

"Bulgaria."

As she looked at him with flashing disbelief, he responded with another guilty cough; he had obviously been caught in the act of... what was the opposite of exaggerating? "So I admit to makin' a coupla moves in that direction, thinking she might be missing her guy, but didn't get very far, if you get my meaning. So after a few things happened, I backed off."

"What kind of things happened, if I may ask?"

"Maybe just a little love play. Some heavy breathing an' stuff. But she thought better of it. Me too. Me bein' also a good faithful partner ...basically."

"That's good to know." There was a heavy note of sarcasm in her voice.

"But maybe she likes Roddy the Body better!" Krish winked as if to say: if that's the case, let's get some bodily revenge going here.

She was starting to think her deal to nurse, as well as put up (with), this broken would-be superstar might be giving him the wrong idea. Especially as some of the nursing could be horribly close-up. He did his required business into a basin and a bottle, which she was obliged to remove and flush away. Even worse, he had to be kept clean. So she had to wash his back and other unreachable areas every day – but drew the line at shaving his chin and getting down to his Elvis pelvis – reminding him that his own arms still worked.

Nonetheless, this degree of physicality was subconsciously creating a familiarity that could go one of several ways – fondness, indifference, full-on sex, or simple hatred.

Teasing her about Roddy's temptations wouldn't help on the fondness front. When added to his dislike of the healthy brunches she brought him after her late-morning sleeps –

smashed avocado on rye and standard English morning tea – the nascent relationship was on shaky ground. She relished the tea anyhow, and on taking one last gulp before heading out, she mused that maybe she didn't have time to do two nursing shifts in a day... "plus all the shopping Roderick once dealt with through Morrisons". She was grateful, at least, that his dog was temporarily off her hands, she thought, when...

The doorbell rang. A soft ping-pong that had always irritated her but no more so than at this moment.

She opened the front door to neighbour Willie, also bearded but very grey, of face and hair. Bespectacled as he was, he couldn't help noting she was clutching a bottle of whisky. At this time of day! He was gripping the dog's leash in one age-wrinkled hand and a big envelope in the other. The dog was bouncing and tail-wagging with the thrill of being back on home territory, Willie looked less delighted. "Yes, Willie?" she almost snapped at him.

"Sorry to bother you, Fiona," he said. "But I've got a couple of things for your attention."

"Not Shep, I hope," she said, patting the eager dog's head. "We just can't handle him at the moment. I thought you said you could keep him for..."

"Aye, it's about him. I might have to hand him back sooner than we thought, as the hospital says I'm due for what they call a procedure. Dodgy kidney, you know."

"When?"

"Four weeks from now," he said.

"Oh, I'm sorry. For you! Not me. Though that could be challenging for us both. What's the other thing?" She pointed at the envelope.

"It's a get-well-soon card for Roderick. From me and all the neighbours who know him. We're all concerned about him.

Nobody's seen him around lately. You said he was indisposed..."

"Did I?"

"And some of us saw an ambulance at your door. But no sign of Roderick being out and about since. So we're just wondering. And Shep is missing him like crazy. Can I ask how he is?"

Before she could answer, Shep broke free and raced into the house. He poked his nose into every room until he got to Lorna's. Shocked at the bearded body in the bed that didn't smell anything like Lorna or any of his family, he started barking hysterically and pulling at the bedclothes.

"Down boy, get down!" shouted Krish in a voice more angry than sympatic to Shep — who kept growling until the others appeared behind him.

Mouthing "sorry" all round, Fiona parked the whisky bottle on the nearest surface she saw — the control panel of Lorna's electric keyboard — while pulling the dog away, calming him down and handing him back over to Willie. Who sniffed the whisky-scented air and looked bemused.

An explanation was obviously expected.

"Willie, this is our house guest, Krish Ray," said Fiona. "He's Roderick's friend in need of temporary nursing care. The ambulance was for him. He's got a badly broken leg."

"Oh, hello, I'm sorry to hear that," the old man said, turning to Krish. "I do the dog lodging. So where's Roderick then?"

"He's off on business," offered Krish, knowing the Elvis story wouldn't be believed.

"We believe he's in Sofia," said Fiona, once more with feeling. "Bulgaria."

"Oh. I've been there," said Willie, a one-time merchant seaman. "Once stopped off with cargo at Varna. Sofia is beautiful."

"Yes, we know that," said Fiona curtly as she ushered Willie and Shep out the door. "How well we know that."

"Better give this to your lodger then," said the old man as he turned back to hand over the card.

Somehow, she knew. And he knew. The Avenue was now primed to erupt with gossip.

Chapter 21
Sensitive relationships

"Cheers, baby!" he hollered when he heard the front door opening. A shout so loud Fiona feared the now-eagle-eyed neighbours might call 999. Relationships were getting fraught within their tricky triangle. Not just because of the whisky incident, though that surely contributed...

She had come home to a well-tippled Krish stinking of the stuff all over his body, duvet and bed. Somehow, he'd managed to reach the Scotch bottle on the keyboard but hadn't, after taking his fill, managed to replace it. It had slipped from his grasp and crashed to the floor, spilling its broken glass and contents liberally around the room. And even as she took in the shocking scene, he slurred out a demand that he should be bathed and changed there and then. When she refused, with a brief "in your dreams", a tsunami of bitterness cascaded out...

Resentment of his incarceration: "I might as well be in San Fucking Quentin. I never see the light of day in this miserable little room. You should stick me out in the freezing garden.

That'd be more fun. I'm bored to death in this godforsaken country."

Dependence on a woman who wasn't 'his': "Who are you anyway? A mercenary bitch, that's who. You kinda look after me for cash but you ain't got the a cent's worth of care for who I really am. Deep down under the Elvis thing, I'm just a guy who needs a friend. And all you ever think of is your precious Roddy. Who maybe ain't thinkin' of you no more."

Distance from home and culture: "I bin away too long from my happy ole apple pie world. I got an SMS message from my girl today. Saying she'll find another guy if I don't get home soon. At least for a coupla weeks. She's even more of a love-starved bitch than you."

Most intensely, the 'snatching' of his Elvis role: "As if losing my job wasn't bad enough luck. I don't even know if your Roddy's gonna keep my headliner spot forever or what. Oh, Lordy in the great big sky, why don't you gimme a break?!"

In the light of another day, of course, he was full of remorse. He put his hands together in praying position and begged her: "Please forgive me. I know not what I do. Especially under the influence." He tried the smile again and it seemed to work a little. He thought he saw a degree of forgiveness in her eyes as she came forward with fresh bedclothes. But he also saw how much he'd hurt his carer and wanted comfort her by gripping her arm. She pushed the arm aside, saying he'd have to get up and change his sodden bedclothes and pyjamas himself.

"Get up? How can I do that?" he protested.

"Wait a moment and you'll see," she said.

She left the room for a few seconds and returned with a big, robust-looking wheelchair, carrying a crutch and boasting an extendable platform upfront to take an elevated leg. Krish's eyes widened like those of a child shown a Christmas present. And this time, the smile was genuine.

"The doctors thought you could start this now," she said, showing him the brake and clicking it on. "So I'll help you into it then leave you to it. It's top of the range. It'll take you anywhere you want. In the house anyway. To the loo, for instance, to do your own personal stuff... like shaving and changing and whatever else you guys do in there. Even into the freezing garden you were so sarcastic about."

He swung his legs out of the bed in a sudden reprise of the one-time action man. Even the sharp arrow of pain in his injured leg was ignored. He stood up shakily with the help of the crutch and she gathered him around the shoulders as he half-fell into the chair. "Feels great!" he said, and neither of them knew if he meant the touching or the fit of the seat.

But before he could learn the forward, back and steering techniques to start zipping around in his new-found joy, more remorse was called for ...literally. His phone buzzed. It was Roddy, having talked to Fiona about the whisky incident. "I hear you been givin' my lady a hard time, buddy," said the Scot, realising he was talking Elvis-style again. He added, in his own accent. "I am rather hoping you will apologise profusely, or I'll have to..."

"Or you'll have to what? I have apologised, Roddy, and she has graciously accepted."

"I'm very glad to hear that."

"I know I done wrong. I'm saying sorry to you too. If only for the godawful mess I made of your spare room carpet."

"That's not important to me. Fiona is important to me. I know she's taking good care of you, but you should be looking after her well too, while I'm away."

"Of course I am."

"In the nicest possible way, if you know what I mean. I hope you're remembering she's mine."

He didn't mention he'd forgotten that, only a few minutes ago, and the Presley song *I Forgot to Remember to Forget* popped into his head. "I promise to remember, pal, if you don't forget the headliner job you're doing is mine. When I have your carer and you have my career, mutual respect is the name of the game. To quote the man himself, we can't go on like this with suspicious minds."

"No, we can't."

"The tour should be finishing quite soon, yeah?"

"Yeah. Less than three weeks to go, I reckon, by which time you should be up and running again, and I should be back home in dear old Scotland wi' ma ain folks. It's been a great old experience but I'm getting hellish homesick."

"Join the club, Roddy. When you get back here, I hope to be on a plane to Boston. The team will surely have another tour planned, but before I join it, I'll get a quick whiff of my own little lady's perfume and my own home air. So I maybe I won't see you."

"In case we do meet again, I won't say bon voyage yet."

"Okay. Bye for now then. And I suppose I should say thanks for filling my cowboy boots."

"And I should say thanks for giving me a leg up."

"That ain't funny, pal."

"Byeeee."

Choosing not to listen to their exchange, Fiona had made herself scarce... visiting Willie with some food for Shep. Who wasn't satisfied with a few titbits. His eager, smiling face also demanded a long walk, down by the seaside, during which she checked her bank balance electronically. True to their word, the ETA show promoters had paid the second instalment of her rental reward. Which rather made all the hassle worthwhile. Especially when added to the sizeable temporary cash injections generated by Roderick. But that would soon be over, wouldn't it? And the money, lovely as it was, would dry up again, wouldn't it? What would they do then?

When she reappeared at the house, Krish had rolled himself back into Lorna's bedroom and lined the wheelchair up beside the keyboard. He was winking and singing *I Can't Help Falling In Love* along to his own accompaniment. And she hoped he didn't mean her.

Or did she?

Chapter 22

Horizons new...or not

"Get your ass up here!" Sam on the Premier Inn phone from one floor above Roddy: "I got some breaking news for you." Roddy groaned into life, struggled from his mid-morning bed and reflected that, as that the next gig wasn't far from Croydon, he could take his time. Especially after another great performance. Evidence of which was still smudged across his cheeks and neck. Exhaustion – he excused himself in the shaving mirror – had clearly beaten the need to clean off the fans' lipstick.

"What could be so bloody urgent?" he asked his own reflected face, as he padded it almost clean and noticed that, unusually, the red smudges – some of them pretty purple – spread down his neck to his chest. He was still almost wearing the now-crumpled white jumpsuit and tried to remember why he'd been so knocked out. By more than tiredness? Had he been drinking? The graphic images that swept across his addled brain were obviously from another wet dream about her ...weren't they? Couldn't have been real. He'd never been one for actually picking forbidden fruit.

He filled the room's kettle and set it to boil, intending to grab an instant coffee. But the phone rang again, offering only a repeat of the first exhortation. "Okay, okay," he said, cradling the phone as he grabbed a dressing gown, abandoned the coffee, and slipped sockless feet into his day shoes.

Sam's door opened even before it was knocked on. One of the English backing girls summoned Roddy in with a toothy grin, then he saw the others. All excitedly gathered around the boss, who was holding court from the big pillows of his king-size bed. What was going on here?

"Have you guys been having an all-night orgy or what?" asked Roddy, realising he was speaking with an American twang and immediately revising his thought, noting they were all fully dressed. Must have been a pretty boring party...

"Maybe it was you havin' an orgy," said Sam. "You look kinda zapped out."

"Do I?" Roddy ran his fingers through his own tousled hair. "Sorry."

"Take a seat, ma boy," said the boss who, after Roddy squeezed on to a sofa spot beside Sofia, went on: "No, we ain't been ravin' here all night, just for an hour or so; but there was a good reason why we didn't invite you to begin with."

"Oh, why's that?" Roddy had already sensed this moment would be relevant to his future. But even if he were fired with a few more dates to go, it wouldn't be a big deal. He'd had a brilliant time. The venues he'd rocked after Edinburgh – Newcastle, Derby, Nottingham, Guildford, Chester, Wolverhampton, Manchester, Liverpool, Blackpool, and many more – swirled through his head like the panels old movies flashed on screen to sum up time passing. How could he be sorry? Now two-thirds done, the tour hadn't been just artistic fun but socially and financially rewarding. He'd made great money and great friends, especially the two fellow-Elvises and his compatriot Hamish. Maybe even Sofia. But if he was true to himself, he was growing ever more homesick, missing and worrying about Fiona (and Krish).

But there was one more potentially troubling psychological reason for thinking tour termination wouldn't hurt too badly...

He knew that, if he wasn't careful, he might soon believe (as the fans did) that he was The Man Himself. He was beginning not just to sing like him, but to talk and think like him. Indeed, in trying to establish collegial friendship with him, Krish had called him twice, and warned him of this; told him he must remember the adoration belonged to Elvis the Pelvis and not Roddy the Body. Otherwise, a kind of madness would take over...

"We didn't invite you at first," said Sam, "because we been havin' a vote about the tour's future make-up. A whole 'nother tour in fact. The promoters tell me they wanna do Europe after the UK. Which raises a serious kinda question re our third Elvis, if I can put it that way."

"A vote?"

"Yeah, with due respect to Krish, I reckoned we had to ask the whole goddamn company to state a preference – you or him – assuming he'd soon be back on his feet. It was all anonymous. In this room half an hour ago. Blind voting. Unsigned scraps of paper in a tea-pot. The idea was, whoever was favoured by the boys and girls who'd be working with you, he'd be asked to join us for three months in Europe."

"And? Who got the thumbs up?" Roddy had a flashing fancy of himself dressed as Elvis in US army uniform in Germany.

"Well, I have to say it was you, ma boy."

"But I..."

"And in view of that, we need to know if you'd be up for it."

"What about Krish?"

"To be blunt, I reckon that depends entirely on you. If you go for it, we'll retire him. If you don't, we'll rehire him. Sure, you pipped him at the post, but we all know he's pretty damn good too. He's just a more complex, cussed character."

"So Krish is a Jack the Lad."

"Eh?"

"It's a British expression, I suppose, for a bit of a chancer."

"Eh?"

"A cowboy."

"Okay. But it's a happy kinda problem – for us anyhow; though maybe not for Krish if he's left out."

"Phew," said Roddy. "I'll need to have a damn good think about that."

"You think on," said Sam, pulling himself up off the bed with a sigh. "But don't take too long. We're all gonna find ourselves a bite of breakfast. See you downstairs?"

The whole party-that-wasn't trooped out and left a perplexed Roddy sitting on the sofa with Sofia. She looked into his eyes sympathetically and pulled a wipe from her pocket. With it, she began to remove from his neck some lipstick marks he had missed.

"I came to your room last night to clean your face, as usual," she said, "but you didn't answer my door knocking. Must have been asleep already. So now I do what I can with your handsome face."

Roddy laughed. Now it wasn't just The Body that was

149

registering female admiration; it was The Face. But was it really *his* face they seemed to like? Or it was Elvis Presley's? There seemed no way of knowing, although he did get the feeling that Sofia – being professionally part of the great deception – was more inclined towards the real human being sitting here in some awe of her. Of her invisible mending and artistic make-uppery, he meant. But maybe also of her own make-up ...of purple lips, silver-blue hair flecks and matching nails climaxing the long, sensuous fingers.

As she worked lower and lower removing the purple smudges, his body quivered uncontrollably. "Please..." he pleaded, not knowing whether he meant stop or go on.

"Do you fancy doing it then..." she began.

"Well, I'm married," he flustered.

"...the Europe tour?" she clarified.

"Oh," he stuttered. "I'm not sure."

"I am European, you know."

"I know."

"From Bulgaria. If we go all the way..."

"All... the... way?" The three words seemed far apart from each other as he tried to control his quickening breathing.

"All the way near there; if the tour goes all the way to my country." That sweet, enigmatic smile again. "I could show you my home town of Sofia, after which I was named."

"That...would...be...nice."

"Sofia can get very warm sometimes," she whispered, loosening her collar and closing her soft breasts up tight to him. "In the summer. Can be very hot. Sofia is beautiful."

Roddy sighed. "Oh, I know, I know," he said, sure he was seeing his own delicious confusion in her luminous blue eyes.

And she chuckled a little as if she knew too.

Breakfast might have to wait a little, they both reckoned.

Chapter 23

Man meets mountain

"Grrrrrrrr." A combined growl and cough. Now Krish could eject himself from the wheelchair and twist his body round. Just as he was doing now, transferring himself and his huge plaster leg into the little Polo that had been looking at him for the two days of his new mobility. Fiona seldom used it to go to work, so it just sat there. Seeing it was automatic, he figured that, if he could get into the driver seat and elevate his heavy left leg across the passenger seat, his right foot could do all the work for highway locomotion and local touring.

Fiona wouldn't like it if she ever found out; neither would the police department, but...

But he would. A grand tour wasn't on, of course, as the further he took it the more dangerous the exercise would become...facing a serious accident, or worse, Fiona's wrath. He had heard, however, that Edinburgh was quite a scenic place while also being quite neat, so he'd limit his jaunt to a couple of miles. Enough to give it a chance to counter his "godforsaken" description.

His new confidence had begun with the fridge; when he realised he could reach up and into it without leaving the wheelchair. While he didn't want to clean it out, like a thief in the night, he couldn't resist the little pack of French cheeses Fiona was obviously partial to. Little slivers at a time and she wouldn't even notice, he reckoned. But crumbs on the worktop were, or would be, unwanted evidence of this minor offence. So he opened a lower cupboard in search of a cleaning cloth and there, hanging on the back of its door, was the car key.

It was even more tempting than the cheese.

So here he was. Turning it, turning it, and feeling his heart jump with the firing of the little engine. Being American and used to automatics, he reckoned moving the car out of its garage's approach drive and into the street would be a doddle. Not quite. It lurched forward and back, like a bronco at a rodeo, until he tamed it like the real cowboy that he was.

He could have turned left on the main road and found the Forth, but he chose right, forgot to keep left and incurred the honking anger of three local drivers. Escaping miraculously, he found, to the delight of his widening eyes, that he was incredibly near to the city's central mountain. Not only that; it was possible to drive all over it. On a high road that could make the most sensational Formula One track. With which thought, he was beginning to get the hang of the car and throwing it round the bends in a flourish...before stopping near the rocky summit to admire the cityscape.

He pulled himself out of the car and, holding on to his extended safety belt...walked! Not much, a few tentative steps, but enough to get give himself a great picture of the place. "Awesome," he gasped, and for once he really meant it. This was surely one of the few cities in the world that had not been raped by tall matchboxes reaching to the sky. This was a skyline of fine old buildings punctuated by dramatic church steeples stretched between the book-ends of a palace and a dramatic castle, that had probably changed little in three or four centuries.

He fumbled his phone from his top pocket and asked for some facts about "Edinburgh's central mountain". The answer came...

He was in the Queen's Park standing on Arthur's Seat, "an extinct volcano thought to be around 350 million years old... the main peak of Edinburgh's central group of hills which rises above the city to a height of 822 ft, providing excellent panoramic views of the city and beyond".

"I take it back," he said to himself, reflecting that he had never stood in a royal park or on a volcano before, dormant or otherwise. "This is anything but godforsaken. God-given, more like."

But there was more. Back in the car after another struggle, the high road took him around the mountain and back down to the foot of the park, where stood – he read again – the impressive neoclassical Palace of Holyroodhouse, the Queen's main residence in Scotland. He wondered if she was at home today; which, for some reason, made him wonder about Fiona coming home later.

The car's hood would not have to be even warm by the time she appeared. But tomorrow was her day off and he would ask her – beg her even – to show him some more of this remarkable place. Perhaps she could even take him somewhere "for a walk". He would suggest to her that he was ready; that he felt he could at least stand on his own two feet.

* * *

Which feet were back on the wheelchair when she began sipping her mid-morning coffee. "Mornin' baby," said Krish the Lad, rolling up to her at the kitchen table, ignoring her grimace, and getting straight to the point. "I was hoping we could maybe have a little runabout in the Polo today. So I could maybe have a walkabout. And take the dog too, so we can make friends."

"A walkabout?" she asked, surprised, as she handed him a coffee mug. "Today? You feel you can do that?"

"I feel I could do anything today." He thumped his chest Tarzan-like. "I'd happily pay the gas."

"You could pay for yesterday's too," she said flatly. "How did you enjoy your little drive?"

"Shit," he spluttered into his coffee. "How did you know about that?"

"The neighbourhood watch," she smiled. "You – or somebody very like you – was seen driving the car away. You were even witnessed bringing it back. When I was phoned about it by ...well, I'm not saying who...there was some amazement at your managing all that with one leg, I have to say."

"Yeah, I'm sorry." That smile again, always appearing during apologies, she noted. "The car was just standing there. I couldn't resist the little adventure."

"It was highly risky."

"I know."

"I can see you survived, though. How is the car? Is she still in one piece?"

"She's fine. A nice little goer if a little slow to get started." He looked her straight in the eye, felt the mischief coming on, and added: "A bit like yourself."

She threw the coffee straight into his face, and he threw his back at hers.

It was meant to be rancorous, but they both found it funny.

They would still be going out for a drive and a walk, it seemed.

Chapter 24

Showdown in the sun

Krish gasped the oft-abused word again, giving back its real power, on seeing the Disneyesque spire of Fettes College reach for the sky. "Awesome! Our old Walt musta been here."

"Not Disney," said Fiona, "but some other famous people were schooled here."

"Like who?"

"Like Tony Blair, the old British prime minister, and even James Bond."

"But Bond wasn't real...was he?"

"No, but his inventor, Ian Fleming, had him going to this college."

He whistled in wonder, as he had at all the sights they'd driven around: the plaques marking the birthplaces of Bond actor Connery, telephone inventor Bell, and boy wizard Potter (the cafe where Ms Rowling created him over cold coffee); the national galleries and museums, Princes Street and its gardens; as well as the castle, Queen's palace and modern parliament building on the edge of the royal park he'd unofficially visited yesterday.

"I really wanna do this for you," said Krish, as they paused at some New Town traffic lights. "Get you over to Boston and show you all the best places."

"Me?"

"I mean you... and Roddy."

"Like what? What's to see there?"

"What d'you know of already?"

"Maybe the harbour where they had the Tea Party."

"Okay, we could start there, but there's also Fenway Park, home of the Boston Red Sox."

"I'm afraid a Tea Party's more my cup of tea."

"Or there's the Freedom Trail, a walking tour of Revolutionary war sites. That was us against you guys. We won."

"Oh, good for you."

"On that subject, there's also Faneuil Hall – the Cradle of Liberty, where all the early planning and plotting went on."

"How interesting." He sensed Fiona wasn't entranced. "Anything more personal to you?"

"Well, yeah! That's gotta be the Regent Theater in Arlington. It's been staging all kinds of wacky stuff since 1916. Including me. It's where I got my first break as an Elvis tribute artist. They've lately staged this guy Doug Church, who I really gotta see in action...performing songs he reckons Elvis would have done if he'd lived on after 1977. Roddy would go for that too. If not you..."

She coughed, as if to concur. "What about shopping?"

"Well, there's Quincy Market. I reckon you'd love that. Boston's shopping and cuisine paradise."

"Sounds fascinating," said Fiona. "But God knows when I...

we...can spare the time. Or the cash. My Elvis is on a finite contract, as you know."

"I'll pay," said Krish. "I'll be up for a new tour soon and the dollars won't be a problem. It'd be great to see you on the other side of the pond."

Before she could respond, Shep barked suddenly, bored with the travelogue and keen to get out walking. She sensed Krish too was ready to walk, so pulled the car into a parking area, not far from where he'd begun yesterday's odyssey. In the volcano's shadow shot through with shafts of sun light. Spring was in the air.

"Talking of ponds," began Fiona, noting there was an actual pond thirty metres away, very pretty with a congregation of swans, ducks and geese. She lowered the window and pointed to it. "That's St Margaret's Loch," she said. "I've got some titbits to feed the birds. Let's see if you can walk around it a little. It's shallow, I think, so falling in shouldn't kill you."

She removed the wheelchair and crutch from the car boot and placed them beside the passenger door. All the while telling the restive, growling Shep to "get down, boy".

"You talkin' to me?" said Krish with a boyish grin as he struggled from car to wheelchair.

"Might as well be," she said, helping him into the seat and gripping the impatient dog.

At the pond's gravelly edge, Shep scuttered around the wheelchair as Krish, helped by the crutch, slowly raised himself out of it and shakily stood beside it. He hadn't felt so much the centre of attention since he was last on stage. Many eyes seemed to be upon him. Not just Fiona's and Shep's. The swans were gathering in expectation of being fed, followed by all the other birds. And there were two families of parents with kids, all apparently focused on him.

As he made tentative step after cautious step, occasionally holding Fiona's shoulders, yet another set of interested eyes appeared without warning. It was Roddy, Facetiming his wife, noting that she was "surprisingly lightly dressed", learning that she was "out for a walk with the dog", and asking for "a view of where you are". She turned away from the others to make a panoramic scan. A surge of jealousy swept through Roddy when he saw not just Arthur's Seat, the swan-filled pond and the dog...but the other man. Yet to get the whole picture – not just the geographic one but the human one – he managed to feign nonchalance.

"Not just out with the dog, I see?" He tried not to sound provocative.

"Yes, also with our friend Krish, who's getting back up on his feet this very minute."

"Our friend? You mean your friend. "

"Well, he's just invited both of us to Boston to say thanks for looking after him."

"Does that include holding his crutch for him?" She looked at her right hand and, as if it was red hot, immediately dropped the support, without which Krish was now managing to limp away.

"Really, Roderick! That's quite out of order. Bloody rude, actually."

"Okay, sorry. I suppose I should thank 'our friend' for the invitation; not that I'll ever be taking it up. Pass him on to me please. I've got some news for him."

"Doesn't sound like a good idea."

"Do it please."

Reluctantly, she handed her phone over to Krish, who was turning back towards her and balancing himself with hands outstretched. One of which took it from her; without ceremony, he shouted 'Hi!' into it.

"I hear I have to congratulate you, Krish," said the disembodied but familiar voice.

"Oh! Roddy! Hi. Yeah, seems I'm up and... well, not exactly running. But walking anyway. So with luck, I should be back in Elvis business in maybe three weeks or so."

"That's when the UK tour is ending, you realise."

"Yeah, but I reckon Sam will have new plans for me. For a new tour." There was no trace of doubt in his tone. It seemed he'd not so much as contemplated the possibility of being dropped from the line-up; or if he had, his way of avoiding it was simply to bury it; in total denial that he ever be replaced by a mere Brit; this particular Brit...

Roddy took a deep breath and said: "I have to tell you there might be some doubt about that."

After a pregnant moment of silence, the question came: "How d'you mean?"

"I mean, there *is* going to be a new tour – of Europe – and the team have had a vote about which of us, which third headliner, they'd like to take with them."

Another silence. A face turning dark with contracted eyebrows, then an explosion: "And, let me guess, they went for you?"

"I'm afraid so, buddy." Roddy tried to sound friendly and certainly not smug.

The blood flooded into Krish's head as he spat out his sudden indignation. "I'm not your buddy, buddy. I don't fucking believe you. But if it's true, I swear I'll seek you out and cut your fucking head off. Just like you've cut my life off."

Fiona stepped forward and tried to defuse the explosion. She grappled the phone from Krish and spoke directly to her husband: "Please, if what you say is true, we have to discuss it rationally."

Shep also sensed the aggro and started whining excitedly at the sound of his master's voice.

"I want to talk to Shep," said Roddy to his wife. "Please point the phone at him."

She was happy to aid the diversion. Master and dog looked at each other on the little screen and, though Shep didn't really register Roddy's image, he certainly reacted – with sheer joy – to the voice he loved most. Panting, whining and smiling with tongue out, he also lightened Roddy's mood, until...

Krish's voice interjected: "I mean it, you bastard. I'll kill you!"

Now Roddy's blood rose. He suddenly saw Shep as his defensive weapon, perhaps even an offensive one. "Attack!" he called out at the phone. The one-time police dog looked around, sensed the ill will in the nearest relative stranger, and pounced. Growling angrily, the dog made a direct hit on Krish's chest and he toppled over into the pond with an alarmed yell, desperately trying to keep his plastered leg above the water. As the swans and other birds made quick, squawking getaways, he sank beneath the surface, dragged down by the heavy but quickly melting leg casing.

Fiona plunged in without a second thought, still holding her phone and ordering Roddy to enlist the dog's help with the rescue her other hand was engaged in: pulling, pulling the struggling figure up out of trouble. "Save him!" shouted Roddy, and Shep obeyed, confused but effective in partly undoing his damage, clamping his big teeth into Krish's shirt and dragging him on to the bank, to lie beside the now-discarded phone.

Had Krish drowned? He seemed to have stopped breathing, and Fiona drew again on her nurse's know-how to give him the kiss of life, lying there on top of him in the sun. He didn't die but it was the last picture Roddy saw on Fiona's phone before *it* died.

A scene that reminded him of Burt Lancaster canoodling on the beach with Deborah Kerr in *From Here to Eternity.*

She had her suspicions...that Krish had overdone the drama to get the most out of her kiss. But when he came to, noting gathering family crowds around the scene, his bitterness had not softened. "The bastard tried to murder me!" he said through gritted teeth, as he mopped up sodden plaster around his leg. "Not satisfied with killing my career, your husband fucking tried to kill me." Fiona looked on blankly, simply not knowing which side to take. But another female voice said: "Are you accusing someone of attempted murder, sir?"

"I sure am," he replied – to a Royal Park Ranger who'd been alerted to the drama by passers-by.

"Can I ask who?"

"Sure can. This woman's husband, Roderick Kirkwood." Shocked, Fiona threw one hand across her face while gripping the still-agitated dog with the other.

"Do you wish me to call the police to get the details and perhaps prefer charges, sir?"

"I sure do," he said.

This is absurd, thought Fiona. He couldn't possibly be serious. She offered their address when asked and thought no more of it. There was a whole new stage of awkwardness to be faced. Not just the physical challenge of getting back to the house, but the further one of now-super-awkward co-habitation. Not for long, however! By the time they got home, Roddy had texted that he wouldn't stand for it. The other man would have to be out in two days. "Haven't made up mind anyway about Euro tour," he added. "You and I still must discuss. All implications of being away so long. If I got so homesick on UK tour, how will I like such a marathon? Could still be his."

Chapter 25

The law's long arm

A pause for thought amid the sound testing. With all its circles and ovals and rich red tones under its famous dome, the Edwardian style of Bristol's Hippodrome wrapped itself around Roddy as he reflected – centre-stage before its still-unfilled seats – on his incredible journey so far. The UK tour almost done, he'd found himself at a crossroads, being pulled in different directions...

He tried to spell them out with his right index finger on the fingers of his left hand:

One – Sam (and maybe even Sofia) wanted to keep him on board for the Euro tour;

Two – Fiona wanted him to come home, finish his "daft adventure" and get a "proper" job;

Three – Krish wanted Roddy right out of the picture;

Four – He himself wanted to go home and practise his new Elvis trade there if possible.

Five – He sensed there would be another consideration. As

it turned out...

With only a week and four more dates to go, he'd promised Sam he would make a decision today so that, among other logistics, the embittered Krish might know his fate. In the event, Roddy needn't have concerned himself on any front; all was decided for him when the cold, gloved hand of a stiff police sergeant landed on his shoulder.

Had the stalls been full, they would have thrilled to the play-like theatre of it. The policeman, boasting a near-Hitler moustache, said: "Roderick Kirkwood?" In response to a stare, a nod and a Presley-style Uh-huh, he continued: "I have a warrant for your arrest. On suspicion of the attempted murder of one Krish Rashid Khan. I must ask you to come quietly. This is necessary to allow the prompt and effective investigation of this alleged offence. I am responding to a request by colleagues in Edinburgh. You are to be escorted there at the earliest opportunity."

"Are you kidding?" said Roddy. "Who the hell's that...oh, him! I'm supposed to have tried to kill him? Is this some kind of joke? Is it my birthday? Are you from a stripper agency or something?"

"Afraid not, sir," said the earnest sergeant, backed by a younger officer who seemed more interested in the female singers starting to hover about the wings, and seemed as if he wouldn't mind stripping off if asked.

"But I just can't go yet," said Roddy, with appealing eyes and hands in praying mode. "I've got a whole set to get through tonight. About fifteen Elvis songs. Surely you can wait in the wings for me to do that. I'm obviously not going to go anywhere but here. I think you'd help me out if you were an Elvis fan."

The older man's rigid face suddenly relaxed into a smile.

"As a matter of fact I am," he said with a flash of pride. "I am a Presley enthusiast."

Roddy saw his chance and pounced: "Got a favourite Elvis song?"

"Yes, actually, as a matter of fact I do. Do you know *Teddy Bear*? That's my favourite. My mother used to sing it to me when I was a toddler playing with my teddy."

"Ok, I'll do it just for you," said Roddy, "if you let me do the set and give me a moment to talk to my boss beforehand. And one phone call to my wife."

The sergeant's smile broadened as he referred to his colleague, who nodded keenly as the girls gathered into a spotlight under test. "Okay," he said, "we'll wait, but the last plane will have flown. So you'll have to stay in a police cell overnight."

Roddy could only laugh ironically. "Bread and water then, is it?"

Cops! The sight of their uniforms petrified Sam for a brief moment – a sign of a misspent youth – before he pulled himself together. "Can I help, gentlemen?" he said, as he pushed his red-jacketed fullness around them them in the pre-show wings. Expecting a story about the use of unlawful drugs. "I'm the big boss man round these parts. Guilty of smoking only the finest Havanas."

Roddy stepped in before they answered. "It's about me, Sam," he said. "I'm being arrested."

"Arrested? For what?" Sam's unlit cigar fell from his lips.

"Attempted murder."

"Eh? You? Of who?"

"Krish, no less. He's accused me of trying to kill him in Edinburgh."

Sam's little eyes widened in further amazement.

"But you ain't been in Edinboro since we..."

"By phone. He says I did it by phone. And dog."

"Dog? Are you fucking kidding me?"

"I set the dog on him by Facetime."

"What? How? Why?"

"I let it slip about the headliner vote – guilty as charged on that one – and he went berserk. *He* actually threatened to kill *me*. I just wanted to give him a fright."

"Jesus Christ. For the love of all that's holy." He turned to the officers and said: "This is surely some kinda... what does Trump call it...a hoax, no?"

Assured that it wasn't, his apoplexy was uncontained. When it finally subsided, he simply said: "I'm sorry for you, Robby. But for me too. What the fuck am I gonna do for the rest of the tour?"

"You haven't forgotten Ken Maybury, have you? The promoter who's my rep in this deal. I'm sure he'd like to see the deal through with you. So I'd bet my cowboy boots his main Elvis, my mentor Johnny Lee Memphis, would be miraculously available as of tomorrow."

"I'll call."

"I already did, five minutes ago. He still has to check but he reckons Johnny Lee will be up for a week down south with three gigs. And Johnny's the best there is."

Sam spread his arms out wide and pulled Roddy into a big hug. Then he actually kissed him. "That's for the help. And it's a fond farewell if our business is done after tonight, as it seems to be. You been fabulous, Roddy! Give us a final show to remember you by!" He walked away, wiping a tear from his cheek.

* * *

"Pardon? You've been detained by the police?" Fiona greeted the news from the theatre's landline with a sardonic laugh. "Attempted murder? I can't believe Krish pursued such a ridiculous charge."

"How could he have got it through?" said Roddy. "Sure, he can report his grievance and get an investigation going; but I don't believe a charge can go ahead on just one guy's complaint."

"I shouldn't think so."

"There surely has to be supporting evidence, other people's corroboration. You didn't say anything to the police, did you?"

"Don't be daft, Roderick. Why would I speak against you? But come to think of it, that park ranger woman seemed awfully keen to see some action."

"That's a thought."

"And I did give her our address. It must have been set up here. While I was at work. When Krish was still in the house on your two days' notice."

"So where is he now?"

"I offloaded him on Willie, to co-habit with Shep."

"How d'you manage that?"

"Sheer bribery − most of this month's rent money. But the police must have come here for details before that. I had no inkling. Maybe he intended to tell me, but I made myself scarce over these days. Talking civilly after he vowed to kill my husband was...well, tricky. You can imagine. But where is my husband now?"

"Bristol."

"Where in Bristol?"

"A police station. Bound for the cells. Courtesy of Avon and Somerset Constabulary. Flying home tomorrow."

"I'll meet you at the airport."

"Thanks, but don't bother. I'm under escort and bound for another cell night, I reckon."

"God, that's awful, Roderick." He could imagine her hand across her shocked mouth. "Truly awful. I told you no good would come of this Elvis nonsense. But who's taking your place then? Krish's nearly walking normally now, I hear, but it surely won't be him, will it?"

"Naw. He won't have his sexy shoogle back yet anyway. Unless you know different…"

"Oh, *please*, Roderick."

"I've suggested Johnny Lee Memphis. He'll probably manage the last three dates."

"That's a good solution, I suppose."

"Yeah. I'll let you know where and when I can be visited. So sorry about this, my love."

"I'm pretty damn sorry too," she said, licking a tear from her upper lip.

Chapter 26

Farewell, my lovely

"Thank-you for the song, sir," said the sergeant. "It was quite... er, touching. However, the time has come, I'm afraid..."

"It's an unfair cop," was all Roddy could say, drying the back of his perspiring neck with a yellow scarf. Before Sofia's voice came from behind a screen.

"I must clean off his face make-up!" she pleaded with the two policemen after they'd escorted him to his dressing room to pick up his "essential stuff".

"Sorry, miss," came the reply. "He's kept us waiting long enough. We must get going back to the station."

"But he has to change his clothes also," she insisted, as Roddy stood back and allowed her to fight on his behalf. "He cannot go out dressed as Elvis Presley."

"That's not a problem," said the other cop, failing to hide a self-amused smirk. "He could really make the jailhouse rock." Noting no applause or even a smile, he pointed to the wheeled suitcase she had packed but left open to swap Elvis suit with leather jacket and jeans. "And would that hold his day-clothes?"

"Yes, and other things like toothpaste, but..."

"We'll take the case just as it is, thank-you miss," said the senior man, signalling to his colleague to close and pick it up. "Unless Mr Kirkwood would like to carry it himself, of course."

"No, thanks," said Roddy. "It used to hold my teddy bear, but I'm into more mature passions these days."

He doubted they'd even got the sarcasm as they hustled him towards the door. He looked back over his high white collar at the tearful Sofia, who had one hand over her mouth, and said: "Farewell, my lovely.."

Her other hand held a little square of tear-dampened tissue scribbled with black ink which she pushed into his retreating pocket. "Please keep in touch," she said, and he was gone.

"Christ, it's Elvis!" exclaimed the desk duty man when they arrived at the station. Roddy curled a lip to enhance the impact. But he didn't want to play; just rest. After the word flashed round the building and the sniggering novelty wore off, he breathed a deep sigh as he was taken below. At last, there was a chance, in the single-bed cell, to shed and pack his precious white creation. And to sleep. And use the toothpaste. Before the odd threesome of rocker and rozzers caught the KLM Cityhopper to Edinburgh at 10.40 in the morning.

In Edinburgh

A moment of mixed feelings for the homecoming Scot. At any other time in any other circumstance, to be around the Police Scotland HQ – in the shadow of Fettes College's dreaming spire Krish had so admired – would be uplifting. Not today. He was about to be prodded by the sharp lances of outrageous fortune, and the offered cuppa wouldn't adequately steel his defence. He was going to need a bloody good lawyer. But he took the tea anyway.

He sipped it half-heartedly as the grim policeman sitting across the interview table read the charge to him formally:

"Roderick Kirkwood, musician, of 88 Vandeleur Avenue, Edinburgh, you are hereby charged with assaulting one Krish Rashid Khan, visiting citizen of the USA, at the Queen's Holyrood Park in Edinburgh, by wilfully instructing your dog to attack him, and thereby attempting to murder him. You do not have to say anything but anything you do say may be given in evidence."

"How? How am I supposed to have attempted murder?"

"By dog, sir, by dog. And mobile telephone."

"Eh? A dog is not a lethal weapon."

"Well, having myself served in the police dog unit, sir, I believe that it is."

"My Shep wouldn't hurt a fly... or even a fly guy for that matter."

"Well, in this case it appears he might have, sir."

"Neither is a mobile telephone."

"Neither is it what?"

"A lethal weapon."

"I might grant you that, sir, but it's the mobile phone is a very recent phenomena so perhaps we should allow the court to make a judgement on that."

"Phenomenon."

"Pardon, sir?"

"Oh, nothing."

"In the meantime, of course, we are obliged to relieve you of said phone. For safety's sake and in case it is needed as evidence. Would you please hand it over to me."

Roddy took the red-framed phone from a top jacket

pocket, laid it flat on the table as if to surrender it, but stopped in mid-slide. "I am surely allowed a phone call...or two?"

"To who, sir?"

"To whom? My wife and my lawyer. Well, I don't actually have a lawyer in mind but I'll ask her to fix one up. She's pretty good at that kind of thing. So I could maybe kill two birds with one call."

Both men's eyes widened as they realised his phrasing was unfortunate under the circumstance.

"I won't be going anywhere while you do it," said the cop.

He waited. They waited. But the call was not answered. Roddy left a message telling Fiona of his location, his predicament, his wish to consult with a good lawyer of her choice, and his need simply to see her. She was obviously dealing with some kind of emergency at work. She would get back, of course... but to whom? And when?

"What now?" asked Roddy as he finished the phone's slide across the table and watched the officer grip it delicately as if it were a bomb as he put it carefully into a transparent plastic evidence bag.

"I have to tell you that the Procurator Fiscal has decided you should appear at Edinburgh Sheriff Court in the morning, and I should warn you that, in view of the seriousness of the alleged crime, the prosecution will be recommending you be fully committed until due course of law... in other words, remanded in custody."

"Tomorrow morning?"

"Yes, sir."

"But I might not have a lawyer arranged by then. May I leave another message for my wife to tell her how urgent the situation is?"

"You will be represented by an on-call lawyer in court.

Sorry, sir, bagged up is bagged up." He pointed at the phone-holding bag but thought twice about tapping it.

"Banged up?"

"Well, that too, I'm afraid. But only for a maximum of one hundred and forty days. Your trial should be fixed before that. Look on the bright side."

Roddy thought better of throwing his cold tea over him and drained it in sullen silence instead.

Chapter 27

An escape route?

"That didn't take you very long."

"What didn't?"

"Getting back to ginger." Fiona laughed. Caustically or affectionately? It was hard to tell. He raked a hand through his red-again hair and grinned wanly, wondering: who is her companion?

To Roddy the jailbird they looked a well-matched couple. Upstanding and professional. Fine-boned, polite and kind to the eye. Both in smart, dark suits. Were they here to help him off the hook or to say they'd fallen for each other in his absence and were running away together?

This wasn't how he'd imagined the happy reunion. Fiona had got to him as soon as she could, of course, but a little too late, and with another woman – the finding of whom had taken time. But Priscilla Robson, a lawyer with a fine reputation as a doughty courtroom defender, was here now. Shaking hands, smiling, sitting alongside her and opposite him at one of the many tables in the huge, hangar-like visiting room at HMP Saughton Prison.

After the introductions, Fiona said: "Priscilla finds the case against you quite absurd and is keen to help us get it thrown out." She turned to the cool beauty with long blonde tresses cascading over her sharply-cut collar: "That's so, isn't it, Priscilla?"

Priscilla coughed lightly, flashed a cuff with a golden butterfly link to cover her mouth, then replied: "Yes. That's so, Fiona." He noticed she wore no other bling; no ring on her long, elegant fingers.

At least his wife wasn't running off with Krish, thought Roddy. But the errant American was to be the centre of their conversation...

"How would you go about that?" asked Roddy, feeling dowdy by contrast in the brown shirt issued to him and another 159 remand prisoners. He fancied the purple shirts he'd seen around, but they were for the (same number of) women; some of whom were sitting about in the cavernous hall meeting their men and their noisy offspring.

"There are a few promising angles we can take," said Priscilla. "The first, of course, is that the basic assertion of the charge – that a dog can be ordered by phone to kill someone at long range – is clearly ridiculous and without precedent. Highly questionable at the very least. And the second is that, thanks perversely to that phone, there is evidence that you acted in justifiable self-defence."

"Explain, please," said Roddy, sitting forward, suddenly intrigued, in his plastic chair.

"The whole episode at the park was recorded on your phone, wasn't it? And you sent the video to Fiona thereafter, didn't you?"

"Eh...yeah. Did I? I'm not sure why."

"So it's now all on her phone as well as yours. The part where Krish says – wait a minute" – she produced a little moleskin notebook and read from it – "I'm not your buddy, buddy. I don't fucking believe you. But if it's true, I swear I'll seek you out and cut your fucking head off. Just like you've cut my life off."

"I think I'm getting your drift," said Roddy, amused at Fiona's flinching on every F-word. Did she ever realise her own name was an F-word?

"And not only that. There's a moment when he says 'I mean it, you bastard. I'll kill you'!"

"I get it. You present this as a case-killer at some point before any trial, justifying self-defence ...is that so? And if it works, the game's a bogey, as they say." He noted Fiona's tutt-tutting.

"That's so. If I can get the Procurator Fiscal to initiate a review of the case on the basis of these points, it might just swing a deal with the Lord Advocate, but I believe one other thing would make it a real belt-and-braces win."

Roddy looked so warily at Fiona she felt obliged to answer his implied question. "We think you should make friends with Krish again and, in so doing, get him to withdraw his complaint that prompted the charge."

A sharp intake of breath and then: "Humph." It was a sound that said oh, shucks, but maybe, if that would help. "So where is Krish now?"

"My spies tell me – well, Willie actually – he's still in the Avenue lodging with him and the dog. But he'll be gone in a few days. With the leg now fully fixed, he's taking the European tour place that you lost."

"Thanks to him."

"You didn't really want it anyway," she said with an

unexpected twinkle. "Admit it. But he's taken it with intense ill will, it seems. The team vote that preferred you has really embittered him. Apparently, he wanted to tell the boss where to put his tour. But..."

"Don't tell me; he needed the work of course, after all those weeks on half-pay."

"That, but also..."

"There's more?"

"According to our snoopy neighbour Willie, Krish recently got a surprise Dear John email from a certain Jodi in Boston. So it looks like his ever-loving, ever-waiting lady back home finally lost her patience. As we know, he had been intending to fly off to Boston to see her when he was all healed up. And now that won't be happening of course. Now that our very unhappy bunny has no personal reason to jump over the pond, excuse the expression; but..."

The lawyer interjected: "But time is of the essence. Even if he wasn't heading off to Europe, he'd have to go anyway. He'll have been on a short temporary visa for a certain event and, now that he's fit enough to fly, questions could even be asked in the next few days. So what do you think? It looks as if he could use a friend, Roderick. Do I meet up with him, say, tomorrow and try to negotiate a truce?"

"Well, yeah, I suppose that has to be a good idea."

"But I'll need some kind of peace offering from you, to show your good will. To suggest there's something in it for him. What could that be?"

Roddy tapped the side of his ginger head and looked to the high vaulted roof. "Well, maybe..."

"Yes?" said the others, full of expectation.

"I still owe him something. Or rather, I still have something of his he should get back."

"What's that?"They enquired in unison again.

"His black jumpsuit. He lent it to me when he came a cropper. Surely to God he'll mention it. He'll really need now, for his new tour. It was all bloody and torn after the medics cut him out of it. But I had it cleaned and fixed. It's in really good nick again. Worth several thousands. If he doesn't want to spend that kind of money on a new one, tell him he can have it back as part of the deal."

"But you said it was only on loan."

"Maybe I misunderstood... maybe I thought it was a gift."

"So where is it now?" asked Priscilla.

"Strangely enough, it's here. In the prison. In the place where they keep the bad guys' stuff. Hasn't moved from the bottom of my suitcase since I was detained."

He clicked his fingers as a crazy idea flashed into his mind. "Maybe Krish can just come here as a visitor and collect it. Then... My white one's in that case too. Maybe we could use them to give the prisoners a double act. Just to seal the deal and repair any friendship we might have had."

The lawyer coughed again and flashed a doubtful, enquiring look at Fiona. "I must say it's a novel thought," she said. "He might buy the returned-suit idea; not so sure about the concert..."

"He'd love it," said Roddy. "I just know it. It would be great practice for him. Before going back on the road."

"Ok, let's try it," said Fiona, to which Priscilla added a nod, before asking...

"Permission? Do you think it would be sanctioned by the prison?"

"Just let me ask," said Roddy, standing up and heading for the door. "I'll speak to the boss right now." He found unit manager Harry Macarthur just around the corner, at the

179

starting line of a corridor that seemed to go on forever. The dark-suited official put away his phone and lent an ear. Two minutes later, he was nodding positively, laughing a little and waving Roddy back to his visitors.

He sat down again, short of breath, clearly missing the lung exercise offered by a forcibly rested rock 'n' roll life. Which might soon, however, get restarted. "The boss says it's probably OK in principle. I think he's a secret Elvis fan."

"Let's go to it then," said Priscilla , standing up with a signal to Fiona and a handshake across the table. "There's no time to lose." Fiona gave her husband a peck on the cheek and a half-smile before thankfully replacing her chair and turning to leave this embarrassing place. Things were looking up.

"Now yer talkin', pal!" Roddy's cellmate was quite a contrast to the just-flown legal eaglet. A man of few words, fewer brain cells and many tatty tattoos. But at nearly thirty, Donnie McTavish was pleasant enough (though less nice behind a broken beer glass). He made Roddy flinch only when the matter of meals came up; he often said with feeling, "Jesus, I could murder a..." There was quite a choice, after all... halal, kosher, vegetarian, gluten-free, good honest traditional... but he wasn't fussy, just ever-famished.

To his credit was a sincere desire to use the prison workshop to better himself "for ma woman and wur wean". He'd gone for joinery as the medium for that and was doing well.

For some reason, Roddy had chosen bike-repairing. The sessions fitted in after breakfast starting at 8.30 and lunch starting around noon. Around 5pm, they were back at their place in the "halls of residence" – the ranks of cells – ready to try to communicate. Which didn't really mean spoken words; within days Roddy had realised they had little in common.

No shared thoughts on drink and drugs and tattoos. But Donnie liked to listen to Roddy singing, and on this of all days it dawned. "You're fuckin' good at that," he observed. "You should be a professional."

"But I am," said Roddy, yielding to the temptation to boast of his Elvis impersonation exploits, ending with the observation that: "You're talking to Roddy the Body!"

When Donnie had stopped laughing his reddened face off – "Ye've got tae be fuckin' kiddin'!" – Roddy found a moment to announce that, in that context, that he would probably be starring in an Elvis concert for the prisoners "quite soon".

"Now yer talkin' pal!" said Donnie. And within a day, the jail was alive with the excitement of it – fuelled by the workshop's card-making department instantly creating posters with show date and time under the heading:

Roddy the Body & Krish Kay
SING ELVIS

Ranks of old-timers were suddenly feeling young again, as they shoogled along the corridors singing their favourite Presley numbers. The unit manager and governor would soon know there was no getting out of it now.

Chapter 28

Rocking the jailhouse

"Hey, there!" called the unit manager as he spotted Roddy the next day. Both were walking along another long, undulating corridor towards each other through a stream of grey men in various shirt colours – green long-termers, maroon sex offenders, grey short-termers and non-offending vulnerables, and brown remanders, like Roddy. "I have a couple of messages for you."

Roddy stopped to let the tide of humanity roll around him. "Oh, who...?" he started, when the smart-suited official hoved to and began searching the messages app on his phone.

"One Priscilla Robson, a lawyer, says it looks pretty good, Krish has agreed to withdraw his accusation, and she needs a date for his visit and the other thing. I won't try to figure out what all that means."

"I know what it means, thanks," said Roddy through a grin he couldn't hide. "What's the other message?"

"Oh, that's just me passing a message verbally from the

governor. He says we can do the show three days from now."

"That's the date the lady's looking for. Would you mind passing it on to her?"

"As you ask, sir," he said a touch sarcastically. "Anything else I can do for you?"

"Well, there is, actually," said Roddy. "Maybe you can let me see your stage options for holding the show? Assuming you have an idea of how many might come."

"Well, we were first thinking of the chapel, where we tend to hold entertainments like in-house talent events. But when you see it, you might agree with me..."

"In what way?"

"That it might be too small."

Roddy did agree, on scanning at the intimate space with its big central cross in front of a few rows of seats, flanked by religious homilies on posters – such as *Come Unto his Presence* and *I am who I am, yesterday today and forever.*

"Then there's the gym," said the manager. "That's another option."

"How many folk d'you think we can expect?" asked Roddy again, as they approached a big, booming hall, like half a covered football pitch where, with much foot-thumping and excited yelling, a volleyball match was in noisy progress.

"Well, there are around 900 inmates – roughly the same as the number of CCTV cameras around the place – and you'd have to subtract 350 right away. They're the sex offenders, who aren't allowed to attend such events. That leaves 550. Then subtract the non-Elvis-lovers and the can't-be bothered and indisposed, that's maybe another 100. Also, we can't mix the sexes at these events, so the ladies will have to be counted out."

"Eh? They're the biggest fans."

"Aye, it's a shame. It means we're minus another 160. So

we're probably looking at a total of about 300. Which is a lot, actually. More than we've ever had before. Not even the 42-piece Nevis Orchestra pulled in that many. So yes, it looks like the gym'll fix it."

"Talking of sex offenders..."

"Pardon? Oh, very funny."

So the gym it was; three days hence. Next question: Was there enough musical talent in the great airport-like building to provide a backing group? The bikes would have to wait while he found some musicians and, if lucky, some instruments and some time for rehearsing.

The tassled and elaborately embroidered black jumpsuit was parked on the visitor chair beside Roddy when Krish appeared, greeting him like a long lost friend. As if nothing had happened between them. "Hey, buddy!" he boomed out, shaking one hand and gripping his co-star's arm with the other. "We're gonna rock the shit outta this place tonight, are we not?"

"Don't we have some stuff to talk about first?" said a taken-aback Roddy, returning the handshake with a less committed grip. He'd been expecting a more pointed talk about their not-quite-finished dramatic episode.

"Oh, that. We've fixed all that. We reckon it'll all be sorted soon, so you can rest easy about it. Maybe even make a quick getaway!" Krish winked mischievously as he tightened his grip, betraying a certain nervousness not instantly evident in his bonhomie. "Sure, no foolin'...I reckon I ought to eat humble pie and say a big Sorry, Rod, so it's onward and upward from here, my friend... eh?"

"We? Who's we?" As he asked, Priscilla appeared on cue, dressed more lightly than before, and sat down in the same position she had occupied beside Fiona.

"Hello, Roderick," she said. "Fiona asked me to give this to you. Thought you might need it tonight." She delved into her handbag and extracted the old black Cher wig.

"Oh, how thoughtful of you," said Roddy. "Thanks so much."

"Don't thank me," she said. "Thank your good lady. She's the thoughtful one."

"Of course. But about the other thing..."

"Yes," she picked up quickly. "I think we have pulled it off. There should be a final decision about your release in a couple of days if I'm not very much mistaken."

Roddy stood up and shook her hand. "I really have to thank you most sincerely," he said.

She shook her blonde tresses negatively, and took a position that surprised him, considering the identity of the person who first got him into this mess. "Don't thank me," she said. "Thank Krish here, who was good enough to drop his grievance against you. Though he did need some feminine persuasion." She winked first at Krish so Roddy wouldn't see; then at Roddy so Krish wouldn't see. Each sensed, however, that this was obviously a very clever lady of some guile. And the undeniable fact was, she had both men smiling.

"I'm looking forward to seeing you guys in action this evening," she said. "After I've concluded some official business in the management office."

"But women are not allowed at the show, I believe," said Roddy.

She got up, patted down her skirt, and winked again, at both of them. "We'll see about that," she said. "Speaking as a solicitor and not as an inmate, I could be an exception. I might raise it with the governor."

And then she was gone.

"She's quite somethin', eh, Roddy?" said Krish as the ripples of her impact began to settle. "Turns out her mom was a big Elvis fan, which is why she's called Priscilla. She showed me some more of your fair land when we met the other day to talk about you. So now I'm in love."

"With her?" Roddy almost choked on his surprised cough.

"With here. With Scotland." He smiled that smile that could melt even Fiona. "Mind you..."

After a pause, Roddy said: "We've got to talk about the show. I know it's just a bit of fun but we should get it right, no? Though we've performed in the same role, we've never worked together so maybe we should fix some systems. I gathered up a few not-bad backers but we ought to rehearse for an hour or two before the curtain-up."

"If you say so," said Krish, leaning over and grabbing the jumpsuit; caressing it and saying: "Great to see you again, my good friend."

Was he talking to the suit or to Roddy, who prompted: "Well..?"

"Well, I reckon we both know the stuff so well, it shouldn't be much of a challenge. But I won't rock the boat."

"You'd better rock the boat, pal. That's what you're here for."

"Touche," said Krish, with that grin again. Roddy reflected that his co-star didn't look as sad as he should after his Dear John shock. But the prospect of playing Presley always cheered a guy up.

In his boyhood Edinburgh Rock was famous not just for its grand castle but as the inspiration for an eponymous candy bar – of cream of tartar and tons of sugar. But the castle and candy were never as sweet and volcanic as this exercise in retro rockery. Edinburgh had never rocked like this.

The inmates had streamed into the gym to take their seats, full of chattering anticipation. And were not disappointed. There was no wordy introduction. Everyone knew why they were there. Getting straight down to it, the Elvis-suited co-stars launched – inevitably – into *Jailhouse Rock*, taking verses in turn, with some harmony to close. The formula was instinctively adopted for all the numbers, as the mood of sheer foot-thumping excitement grew with each note blasted out from the stage. From *Hound Dog* through *Heartbreak Hotel* to the one that seemed to have some poignancy for the singers... *The Girl of My Best Friend*.

But unpredictably, it wasn't an Elvis song that sealed the deal. They had discussed the idea and practised it with the four backing musicians; but no-one was sure it would work inside a Presley theme. The audience seemed go with it, though, as Roddy stepped forward and said: "As most fans will know, Elvis was a big fan and friend of a guy called Johnny Cash. A fellow member of the Million Dollar Quartet, actually. And Johnny was famous for a song he sang for the prisoners of Folsom Prison in California. So I'd ask Krish, our resident man-in-black American, to kick this one off and I'll join in as we go along..."

Hardly a word was sung before the cheering started. Krish found his deep Cash voice too, and trembled it out to ever-louder cheers and applause...

> *I hear the train a comin'*
> *It's rollin round the bend*
> *And I ain't seen the sunshine*
> *Since I don't know when*

* * *

It wasn't just Roddy who joined in as it rolled along. Every voice in the hall seemed to be on board that train a comin'. And when it finished, the applause went through the roof. Feeling pretty proud of himself, Krish scanned the back of the hall in the hope of seeing Priscilla, but she obviously hadn't managed to negotiate admission.

"I think Elvis would have approved of that," said Roddy. "So let's call it a day there."

They both bowed, thanked their musicians, and took their leave to a huge chorus of "more!"

The band refused to move and, along with the entire audience, waved them back on the crest of a tsunami of cheers and whistles.

"Ok, let's give them something optimistic to end on," said Krish, pulling Roddy back to centre-stage. "Somethin' that says there's another better day comin'."

"Yeah we all want that," said a yielding Roddy.

"What do you reckon then? Got a fittin' number in mind?

"Reckon so," said Roddy as he stepped forward with a starting chord that the boys picked up right away. Then they launched into it with all the Elvis energy and style they could muster....

> *When my blue moon turns to gold again*
> *When the rainbow turns the clouds away*
> *When my blue moon turns to gold again*
> *You'll be back within my arms to stay*

When the double act came to a perspiring, breathless finish, there were even more shouts demanding an encore. They were silenced only by the manager stepping on to the stage to say: "Don't worry, gentlemen. We'll have them back again very soon."

As Roddy finally climbed down from the stage, he thought he might have to hold the boss to that, even though Krish was about to leave the country.

Chapter 29

Three's company

"I thought you guys were great together!" No-show Priscilla suddenly appeared, ready to drive Krish away, after all the back-slapping inmates had trooped out. She stood at the exit beside the manager, who agreed: "Yes, it went well, I must say. So if we want you back for a repeat performance... in view of developments, I must ask: Who's your agent?"

The two still-perspiring Elvises looked at each other, and Roddy said: "We'll have to get back to you on that."

Krish turned to Priscilla and asked: "How did you see the show? We didn't see you in the hall."

"Ah hah! She smiled and playfully touched his nose with her car key. "A little light persuasion, my lad." Roddy's eyes widened at this brazen display of ...was it affection? Whatever it was, it was beyond the call of professional duty. "Saw it on CCTV. The management kindly allowed me to sit in on the monitors. And I've taken a little video from that. The quality won't be to write home about. But you can check it out with me sometime."

She took him by the arm and said: "Let's go."

Roddy called after him: "Cheerio then. Maybe we'll meet again for another session some day? Thanks, buddy."

"Maybe baby," said the disappearing Krish, about to be followed by the manager seeing them out; who observed: "Thanks, buddy...maybe baby. They're familiar words. Who...? "

"Buddy Holly," said Roddy. "Elvis has left the building."

That Elvis sure, though not yet the resident one. But just as Roddy the rocker was becoming the jail's established star, celebrated in every department, it was time for more goodbyes – when his get-out-of-jail card was played; when, as expected, the case against him was officially declared unsafe and aborted.

Was that a tear he saw in the eye of cellmate Donnie asking for an autograph? Was it a tear the cell-ebrity felt in his own eye as his not-bad backers sang Vera Lynn's *We'll Meet Again* to him? Before he could leave, his right hand was sore from all the firm handshakes of well-muscled men.

And then he was out...

Sitting on his big suitcase before the glass-fronted entrance of the sprawling modern building awaiting Fiona in the Polo. Waiting and waiting...

When half an hour had passed, he unzipped the case and fished out his mobile phone. Before it vanished with the last of the charge, he saw her brief text: "Sorry I can't be there for you. There will be others."

His heart slumped. What did that mean? Was she abandoning him on the very edge of his new freedom? She'd been active in springing him and now she was happy for him to find "others". For what? To share his life? His great-escape elation vanished like sun-hit snow as he began to realise just why she might feel like that about him...

The respectable day job had long since gone.

The "daft adventure" into Elvis impersonation had bitten the dust.

Its temporary injection of money would soon dry up.

There were no serious prospects of a decent income any day soon.

She might have a point, he conceded. He'd just presumed she would keep their heads above water while he mucked about some more, vainly seeking rewarding endeavour. But he was getting on a bit; what realistic chance did he now have of doing them proud?

He sighed deeply, overwhelmed with gloom, as he hauled himself up and headed down the drive towards a bus to take him home. Home? Did he have one any more? At least he would have to clear up his stuff before seeking pastures new. Or before maybe just calling it a day. He imagined picking up the dog and "family" car and taking them to a high cliff over which they could simply drive...and be no more trouble to anyone. "All my trials soon be over..." he groaned, in the words of the song.

But what, talking of cars, was this? An enormously long pink automobile with fins that would impress a shark suddenly swung across his path and screeched to a halt inside the car park. He turned and walked towards it, driven by curiosity. He could see it was a Cadillac; probably a Fleetwood from the 1950s; the model Elvis bought for his mother when he first had a few hits. The model he'd seen several weeks ago in Labinjoh's car yard. Was he dreaming? He thought he saw two guys in the back seat who looked like Elvis in shades.

Suddenly the car's roof came down and the two Elvis lookalikes raised their arms in greeting, both wearing plain clothes but wide grins. "Hi, Roddy!" they hollered in unison.

One of them was Krish, the other Johnny Lee Memphis. The released jailbird walked towards them, with an uplifting heart.

"Hi, guys, this is quite a surprise," he said. "What's going on?"

"Jump in," said Johnny Lee, making room for him in the back and parking his suitcase in the front passenger seat. "We're taking you home."

At which point, Roddy clocked the familiar face of the driver. Under another pair of shades, it was recognisably Ken Maybury of GLK Promotions. He turned around and shook Roddy's sore hand enthusiastically. "Great to see you," he said.

"To what do I owe this honour?" asked Roddy. "I had just assumed our business was concluded."

"Far from it," said Ken. "I have had this absolutely stonkingly brilliant idea and you are set to be key to it. Along with these other would-be Elvises, of course. Cripes, have you ever seen such a car..."

"No never," said Roddy, touching the chrome ashtray in front of him. "Not in the pink flesh anyway. A Fleetwood isn't it?"

"Carload, I was gonna say. Have you ever seen such a carload of talent in your life? I sure as hell haven't!"

"No, come to think of it, neither have I. So what's the reason for this ...er, stunning gathering?"

"It's to pin you down to a contract for my great inspiration. We could've had a formal meeting in my office, but this is such a Cadillac of a project, I had to set it up in a matching rock'n'roll vehicle. Only hired, but pretty glam, eh?"

Johnny Lee interjected: "He wants to know about the proposed deal, Ken." As Roddy nodded thanks, Ken resumed...

"OK, here's the deal." Ken turned fully to address the trio. "It started for me with the question: Why should the Yanks have it all their own way with their three-star Elvis spectaculars? We have at least two Scots who can deliver the goods on that front, to set up something in competition. Namely, Roddy the Body and Johnny Lee Memphis. And now, to complete the set, we have a third guy, who is actually an American and a veteran of the original show. I believe you know each other, Roddy...So I don't need to introduce you to Krish Kay."

"Hi!" said a bright-smiling Krish.

"Hi! Good to see you again so soon," responded Roddy. "But I don't get it. You're supposed to be heading for Europe on Fantoni's latest tour."

"Yeah," said Krish. "But frankly, I didn't like being the second choice – after you – though, as you know, I did reluctantly agree. Until this opportunity came along. To be part of a threesome based in Scotland. On the same kinda money. So I told Sam where to stick his offer. Right up his..."

"Ah, so you'll be working out of Scotland?"

"Yeah, my new love!"

"In that case, what'll you do about a work permit?"

Ken stepped in here with an assurance that "we've got that in hand". Explaining that although Krish probably wouldn't qualify for a straightforward permit, a plan had been developed with an "alternative" option. A good lawyer was already working on it.

"What might that option be?" asked Roddy. "If I'm to be involved, I'd like the operation to be all above board."

"It's a fiancee visa," said Krish. "That's what we're applying for."

"But you need a fiancee for that, surely?"

"Yeah."

"Do you have one?"

"Well, yeah. As Ken says, we've got a good lawyer dealing with it. Someone you might know."

"Oh, Priscilla then."

"Reckon so." There was something about the look he exchanged with Ken that made Roddy ask: "Is she more than your lawyer perhaps? Maybe your fiancee too?"

"Well, yeah,"

"Bloody hell. That was quick."

"It's just a technicality, Roddy. She's just putting her name on the line to ease the deal for me. But who knows? Maybe we can make a go of it. If not, she can pull out at the altar if she wants to after six months. If I read her right – well, read her T-shirt actually – she reckons good girls love bad boys. So I think she kinda goes for me but also sees me as a kinda gift to her Elvis-crazy mom. To the extent of mom finding a back room for me."

While Roddy sat with astonished mouth wide open, it was back to Ken again – to outline the master plan. If Roddy agreed, his company would have three ETAs on the books, satisfying the ever-growing demand Johnny Lee was struggling to meet. Each would do maybe two solo gigs a week at £500 each and every fortnight or so, Scots and North of England theatre diaries permitting, they'd get together to mount a Three Ages of Elvis yielding £1000 each. That worked out at £6000 a month, Roddy quickly calculated. "Even Fiona would be pleased about that kind of regular salary," he let slip.

"Oh, she knows," said Ken. "She's kind of party to this."

"Eh? How?"

Krish answered with one word: "Priscilla."

"Oh," said Roddy. "So may I ask if my wife expects me to sign?"

Johnny Lee answered: "She does, I think. Because – did you hear that? – we intend to limit the Big Mac spectaculars to Scottish and the North of England cities. With the great advantage that we can all maybe make it home most nights. She seems to like that idea. We thought you would too. It's the nearest an Elvis tourer can get to a nine-to-five job."

"Reckon you're right," said Roddy, thinking that levels of on-the-road temptations were probably directly relatable to the length of the roads in question. "It would surely be good for my marriage."

"Only we're not going to call them Big Mac spectaculars. That's just a working title. Though we're mainly Scots, we won't stress that. We'll still project the American Dream even though the audience might be complicit, the way they accept you guys are not really Elvis, but... We know you were claiming to be from Dallas, Roddy, so we'll hold to that. Krish's from the US Boston, so all we still need is an American-sounding origin for Johnny."

"I've been thinking about that," said Johnny Lee. "I live in Stirlingshire which is as near as dammit to Renfrewshire, where there's a village called Houston."

"Houston?" said Ken. "I don't have a problem with that."

"Oh, crivvens," said Johnny Lee. "Let's get this show on the road."

Chapter 30

Sign on the line!

The big beast burst into life and took off again, Ken panting as he fought the thin left-hand steering wheel that demanded sheer muscle power. He'd thought the "get this show on the road" exhortation pertained to the car, while Johnny Lee had meant the actual show. As they stopped at a traffic light, he spelled it out: "I meant let's get the lad to sign now... or not."

"Understood," said Ken, "but we can talk as we go." Going meant running a gauntlet of public attention as the shocking pink leviathan pushed on through the leafy, daffodil-lined Meadows towards Portobello. Even when those on board couldn't hear them, the ooohs and aahs of passers-by were easy to discern behind their pointed fingers.

"So what d'you say, Roddy?" asked Ken bluntly without taking his eyes off the road. "Are you up for it?"

Roddy was nudged from both sides, before responding: "Ok, do your worst. I can't say I've a helluva lot to lose."

"Yes!" said Ken, snapping his fingers.

"Wowee!" yelled Krish.

"I feel a song coming on," said Johnny Lee. And for no particular reason, he burst into *Lawdy Miss Clawdy*.

It was not yet Festival time, but as the others joined in and blasted the song out over the open Cadillac and into the busy streets, the scene was assumed to be performance art; which in a way, it truly was. Ken drummed his palms on the wheel in time to the song and wondered at how great his threesome sounded together. When he whipped his head round briefly to capture the moment visually, it instantly came to him – the title for the three-man gigs.

"Three amazing dimensions for the three ages of Elvis," he said to himself, editing it down to the way it would appear on the posters with dramatic images of all three stars in action:

ELVISION

The King in three dimensions

He also decided that, for any show, the guys could choose among themselves who'd play which of the ages – youthful rocker, comeback kid or Las Vegas concert star. For all he cared, they could switch repertoires and outfits as the mood took them. That way, role exhaustion would never set in.

But first, the signing.

They were nearing the house and, before Roddy would be free to leave the car, he'd be required to scratch his name on the dotted line.

"Has any of you got a pen?" Ken asked the back-seat trio, having fumbled vainly in his inside jacket pocket.

The others fumbled too, but nothing appeared... apart from negatively shaken heads.

"Oh, brilliant," said Ken.

"It's OK," said Roddy. "Just stop outside the house and I'll pop in for a pen."

The huge machine turned into the Avenue and immediately attracted the attention of curtain-twitching neighbours and a yellow-vested parking attendant. Stopping outside the house was, for the moment, too conspicuous. But Roddy saw that the driveway and garage were free, so told Ken: "It's OK, just turn into the drive and use the garage. I'm sure you won't have long to wait."

Ken strained to turn the Cadillac into the drive but the length and angle of it – as well as its extraordinary width – failed to cooperate. As did the relatively modest width of the gate pillars. Ignoring a nasty scrunching noise and keen to get out of the yellow meanie's radar, Ken pushed on up to the garage ...into which the 1950s Fleetwood simply didn't fit.

One set of twitching curtains was, of course, operated by Fiona. Who would normally have been excrutiatingly embarrassed by such a scene. But she gritted her teeth and came out to greet her man and all his cohorts. "Hello, gentlemen," she said. "I think you had better come in."

One by one, they stepped cautiously out of the stricken vehicle, with Roddy taking up the rear as he collected his suitcase. She held the front door open as they all trooped in, and finally gave her husband a hug and a kiss. At that moment, he simply knew where he belonged.

There was no affected ceremony about it, just a mutual, matter-of-fact understanding that they loved each other. Roderick's absence, combined with the roller-coaster Krish experience, had made Fiona's heart grow fonder and more sure than she'd ever been about their relationship. So much so she'd become resigned to his choice of "career" and helped his management design it into a manageable lifestyle. She knew "career" would always be a word in quotation marks for both of them, but if it made him happy...

"So sorry I couldn't be at the prison gates to meet you," she said, restraining a middle-class chuckle at the statement's absurdity. "I had to go and meet another rather important personage."

"Oh, who?"

"Come and see," she said, trying to keep a serious face when she wanted to grin with good cheer.

She opened the sitting room door, and there they all were – not just Ken and his band of Elvis brothers who'd preceded him, but Priscilla, Willie, some other neighbours, and his faithful, excited Shep being forcibly restrained by a beautiful, tanned young lady. Both of whom rushed forward to greet him. It was Lorna! Showering him with smiles, hugs and laughter as the dog jumped up and tried to get in before her.

"How wonderful to see you," he said. "How was Guate-fucking-mala?"

"Great! Well, effing challenging," she said, moderating her language. "How was prison?"

"Effing challenging," he echoed.

When he emerged from the all-embracing love, he noticed the big banner across the top of the room, which read: *Welcome home, Jailbird!* Under it was a table groaning with peanuts, various nibbles, Fiona's scones, brownies and banana bread ...flanked by three bottles of bubbly and four times as many flutes.

"Before you get tore into this," said Fiona in her best colloquial accent, "there's just one thing you have to do." She signalled to Ken and, as he stepped forward holding some papers, she pushed a pen into Roddy's hand.

Ken cleared a little space on the table, laid the paper down, and said: "Sign here."

Roddy took the pen and, as he signed, said: "Oh, I see. It was all a set-up job."

Cue waves of laughter, applause and Prosecco all round. He couldn't hold back the boyish grin that cleaved his face after its absence of a few stressed years. After all he'd been through it was good, super good, to feel the friendship of his new colleagues, the warmth of his home, and the embracing love of his wife. Fiona had been through a lot too. But both had calculated that mutual acceptance of his now-unusual lifestyle was the price of keeping them happy and financially viable. She smiled back with real love in her eyes.

Uncrunching the embarrassing Cadillac would have to await the end of celebrations.

Chapter 31

A moment in time

"Good morning, Roderick. As a Scot, can you please name for me your favourite Scotch whisky?"

"Eh?" An English voice, yet another of those phone marketeers feigning familiarity. He really wished they wouldn't bother you at the most inconvenient of times. In this case as he loaded the Polo with his first Aldi haul since his great escape. And anyway, only friends and family were allowed to address him by his first name. He would be a bit rude before killing the call.

"Sorry, I don't drink whisky. Not much anyway. And my wife hates it. Good mor..."

"Oh, that's a shame, Roderick. My partner loves it. Which is one of the reasons I'm calling."

"Sorry. Who are you?"

"It's Diana, Roderick. Your long lost sister. I thought you'd recognise my voice."

"Oh, hi!" the tone of his voice changed instantly. "To what do I owe the honour?"

She'd be visiting Edinburgh for the Festival with her daughters, having luckily fixed up a hotel room, and would be buying two bottles of Scotland's best – one to bring back for husband George and another as a gift for the Kirkwoods, on top of a "really special dinner".

"Sounds…shit!" he said, dropping an awkward heavy bag and seeing milk leak out of it.

"Sorry?"

"Sounds wonderful, I mean."

"Which? The whisky or the dinner? And re the whisky, can you please give me a name."

"Both. I've heard tell that Talisker is pretty good. But leave dinner to us. You must come to the house to meet Fiona – and our daughter Lorna, who's just returned from Central America. Not to mention my good pal, Shep."

"Shep?"

"He's a dog."

"Oh, lovely. That would be so nice. The girls love dogs. A real family gathering."

"For the first time. Quite something, eh?"

"What a pity Angus couldn't be there," she said with a sincere tone of sadness.

Roddy chuckled. "Are you sure he'd have liked it? He kept you secret for a lifetime, remember? I can't imagine the old bugger being delighted at everything being out in the open."

"I suppose you're right," she chuckled back.

There was a moment of silence as Roddy gathered his thoughts. "He grew up in the culture of a different, easily embarrassed age. But…"

"Yes?"

"Do you remember the Super 8 film cassette you gave me?"

"Of course. Have you done anything with it?"

"No, not yet. But what would you say to having it processed and adapted to DVD, so we can all watch it on the telly? After dinner, say. That could be fun."

"It certainly could!"

"I have a pal in Livingston who does that sort of thing. VHS to DVD anyway, I'm not sure about his service re film. Not sure either about whether there's sound on the film. I'll get straight on to him and call you back."

The call-back came within five minutes: "He says it's fine, no problem. He reckons it'll be a 50ft Kodak film, in which case the conversion should be possible. He says the original Super 8 films were silent but by the early Seventies some versions had a magnetic strip that could record sound. Let's hope ours is like that. I haven't opened it; too nervous about letting air in or something. He warns it might not be worth it, quality wise, not even counting disappointing content, but..."

"Get his bill sent to me. I'd happily pay to satisfy my curiousity."

"Don't be daft. I'll pick up that tab, and I'll also drive the box to him, and bring it back with the DVD. Don't worry about that either. The gas is on me."

"Tab? Gas? Have you served some time over the pond?"

"I suppose you could say that." He coughed. "Talk again soon."

He packed the rest of his shopping into the car and wondered if he should return to the store for more. But no. There were ten days to go before the visit, and he'd best get guidance from the boss-chef. Or the hostess with the mostest, as Angus would have called her in his day.

* * *

Ten days later

Lorna wasn't over the moon about the sun. It was one of these bright, mid-August days when you could see right across the sparkling Forth to Fife. She had been back for a week, so tanned she hungered for Scottish shade. But delighted to find that, in her absence, she had acquired an aunt, an uncle and two cousins to help her walk the dog on Porty beach. Judie and Gemma were in their early twenties but youthful enough to have boy-band fancies. They were fun – arty, pretty, game for a laugh. And Shep took to them too as they chucked his big yellow ball into the river and shrieked as he retrieved it and shook the river all over them.

In the Avenue garden, the golden oldies were getting to know each other in their own, quieter way: sniffing rose bushes, sipping iced lemonade and exchanging family notes and pictures, mainly digital...but Diana, Roddy and even Fiona were looking ahead to an exciting analogue moment.

It came in the cool of the evening, when the dry white wine had so complemented the superb dinner of Scotch salmon that there was little left of it. Eyes had occasionally landed on Diana's pristine Talisker gift, sitting unbreached in the centre of the table, but no-one had dared touch it. More entertainment was called for nevertheless...

"Let's do it now," said Roddy, standing up and walking over to the TV table, where he found a red sleeve, extracted a DVD disc and waved it at the others as they nursed their desserts and coffee.

"Drum roll please," he said...

A few knives and spoons rattled on their plates as he slipped the disc into the side of the screen and retreated to his seat to activate the remote.

The screen flickered into black-and-white life with a close-up female hand, boasting a snake-like silver bracelet and a big card saying *"Angus on August 16, 1979… exactly two years after Elvis died"*.

And there he was, young and handsome – causing the assembled table to gasp with admiration. First as a fully uniformed kilted piper blowing his heart out… (Sound!" exclaimed Roddy, sending a thumbs-up to Diana). Then as an obviously honoured receiver of a certificate which he held up to the camera, showing the barely discernible words "City of Victoria".

"I reckon that was when his Canadian band did well at the world pipe band championships in Nottingham," said Roddy. "They finished fifth, I think, in the non-UK section."

Another card appeared, held by the braceleted hand. It read: *"Angus later that day, at Isabella's Night Club."*

"I recognise that bracelet!" said Diana, clutching a hand across her heart. "It was my mum's. She always wore it. I used to call it Monty the python."

The card vanished and there was a white-dressed figure in the centre of a small stage. Everyone leaned forward as the figure started to move. The camera zoomed in and it was him all right, with a big Elvis collar and a small band behind him.

"Bloody hell," exclaimed Roddy. "That's Dad in the white Elvis jumpsuit that I inherited!"

"Good Lord," said Fiona …while Diana stared at the screen in disbelief as her father started singing along with his Elvis-inspired moves. "Ssssh!" she urged.

And they all, even the young girls, listened in awe as he began: *"One for the money, two for the show, three to get ready then go man go…"*

Shep recognised the song and started howling.

Roddy became weepy the moment he recognised the song,

which he knew so well. And suddenly recognised a wave of new things about his father. Eclectic shock was a phrase that came to mind.

"That's your grandad," he told Lorna, "and he's pretty damn good too. Was…" And she and her new cousins, bopping to the old rock beat, burst into tears – of laughter.

"Crikey, it really is my Dad," said Diana, wide-eyed with mixed emotions of disbelief, shock and something like pride at his one-time coolness.

And as Angus took his concluding bow to a double round of applause – on the screen and in the dining room – Fiona could only say, as she stretched out to open the Talisker and pour herself a slug: "God almighty, it obviously runs in the family. I need a drink."

Then…

An odd silence. Apart from Fiona breathing out the impact of the whisky on her throat. Everyone at the table looked at each other with an unspoken "wow" on their lips. Until Judie addressed Roddy with: "Let's see it then."

"See what?" he asked, puzzled.

"This famous Elvis suit. As worn by you."

Responding to another drum roll of knives and spoons rattled on plates, Roddy looked at his wife for guidance. But she wasn't even looking back, her eyes diverted by the golden liquid rolling round in her little glass. "You might as well," she said flatly.

Roddy managed a weak smile as he retreated to their bedroom and began to unhook the white jumpsuit that had been given new pride of place in the wardrobe. It was still creased here and there from its last journey, but as he slipped into it he felt strangely comfortable under the high collar and inside the big boxer's belt.

A third cutlery drum roll greeted his reappearance. Somebody gave a wolf whistle. Somebody else said: "Give us a twirl then." And as he was twirling, Lorna said: "I suppose you'd better give us a song too."

"Just a quick one then," he said, and Shep barked with sheer exuberance as his master's voice gave a short introduction – explaining how Elvis had sung other artists' songs, such as the Beatles' *Hey Jude*...which he then launched into...to Judie's delight and Gemma's mock despair.

When it was done, having earned some wild applause, Roddy bowed with a smile and a returned hand-clap before exiting in a warm glow back to the bedroom. And the shock of his life.

Changing back from performer to casual regular fella, he stuck his hands deep into his jumpsuit pockets and found a crumpled-up tissue in the left one. Extracting it to wipe a little sweat from his brow, he noticed some black-ink lettering on it. He unfolded it to read:

Phone me. 00359 2 779828l67. I will find you.

Consumed by curiousity, he picked up his lumberjack shirt from the marital bed, shook it over his his top half, and pulled his phone from its top left pocket.

He pressed the given numbers and waited as they seemed to be buzzing out; wondering if he had read correctly though the smudged ink. But then, a familiar voice said..."Hello. Is that you, Roddy?"

He paused, clutching his leaping heart with his free hand, before answering: "Yes, it's me, Sofia. How are you? Where are you?"

"Where I am is home with my parents, in Bulgaria. I did not go on the European tour because of... well, because I would be missing you, and because..."

"Because what?" Roddy felt the blood surging up through his neck to his throbbing brow. He somehow knew what she was about to say."

"Because I am pregnant," she said.

Roddy fell silent and dropped his half-dressed rear-end on to the bed.

After what seemed like a minute, she said: "Are you still there?"

"Eh, ye-yeah," he said, registering the shaking of his hand that held the phone.

"Who's the father?" he found himself asking, though again he knew what she was going to say.

"Oh, Roddy, how can you ask that?" she said, with deep hurt in her voice.

Suddenly the bedroom door flew open and Fiona was standing there. He closed off the call without another word. But Fiona had some words...

"Why were you on the phone right now when we all want to see you? Not bad news, is it? You're as white as a ghost."

"No, no, just a wrong number," he said. "I'll be right through."

"Well, do get a move on."

As Fiona retreated, he reflected on how much he loved her as he crunched up the tissue note into a tight ball and transferred it to his jeans; from where, he determined, it would be quickly destroyed.

Then he returned to the table, grabbed the Talisker bottle, and shakily poured himself a few large mouthfuls. "I need a drink too," he said breathlessly.

Printed in Poland
by Amazon Fulfillment
Poland Sp. z o.o., Wrocław

63239955R00119